May Wentworth Newman

Fairy Tales from Gold Lands

May Wentworth Newman

Fairy Tales from Gold Lands

ISBN/EAN: 9783337072537

Printed in Europe, USA, Canada, Australia, Japan

Cover: Foto ©Andreas Hilbeck / pixelio.de

More available books at **www.hansebooks.com**

FAIRY TALES

FROM

GOLD LANDS.

SECOND SERIES.

By MAY WENTWORTH.

High as the clouds are the mountains bold
That tower in the glorious Land of Gold,
And cañons dusky with twilight deep
Where a thousand mystic shadows peep.
There are vineyards graceful with trailing vine,
Rich in the wealth of the rosy wine,
There are orange groves and lime trees green
That glint in the sunlight's glowing sheen,
There are deserts yellow with priceless sand,
All these you will find in the Golden Land.

NEW YORK:

A. ROMAN & CO., PUBLISHERS.

SAN FRANCISCO:

417 & 419 MONTGOMERY STREET.

1868.

PREFACE.

In the pleasant Christmas-time I greet the children everywhere.

To some I shall not be a stranger, for we have met before, not face to face, but in the pages of the last year's little book. In the sunny days of childhood, a year is so long a time, that when the summer and winter have passed it seems like an age gone by; yet as again I bring my Christmas offering, I hope to be remembered and welcomed as the friend who loves the children well.

They are the true critics, generous and fearless. For their warm hearts and keen appreciation, I write these stories of the Golden Clime.

May the joy and blessedness of the holy Christmas rest upon them, and follow them through all the sunshine and rain of the coming year.

MAY WENTWORTH.

SAN FRANCISCO, 1868.

TABLE OF CONTENTS.

FAIRY TALES.

THE LITTLE LACE-MAKER.

IT was the happy Christmas Eve, yet it was very cold and dark. Over the quaint old town of Bruges hung the heavy snow-clouds, and the air was filled with snow-flakes, which fell so thick and fast that very soon the ground was covered with a white mantle, quickly hiding the footprints of the few who were still out buying the last gifts for beautiful Christmas trees. Through the narrow streets rushed the wind, shrieking round the corners in its shrill whistle, and seeming to say:—

1*

> "As I go,
> I bring the snow,
> On this holy Christmas Eve.
> Who can show
> Hearts like snow,
> On this holy Christmas Eve?
> Blow, blow, blow!
> Pure and fleecy snow,
> On this holy Christmas Eve."

It was really strange what curious things the wind whistled that night, yet through all ran the refrain of the holy Christmas Eve.

Near the great belfry of Bruges was a stately mansion, where the fires burned brightly in the polished grates with a warm, rosy glow, making upon the wall grotesque shadows of a little boy and girl who were joyous with expectant happiness.

It was early, and the lamps were not yet lighted. The children danced up and down the warm, pleasant room, where they

were to remain until the mother called
them.

The dear, loving mother had been so
busy in the great parlor, doing something
full of mystery, yet the children were quite
sure it was a delightful mystery, that would
bring them a great store of happiness, and
they were luxuriating in their own pleasant
imaginings. The door was still locked, but
the time was fast approaching for the grand
opening.

"I can't wait! I can't wait much longer,"
said the boy, impatiently. "What a lazy
old thing Santa Claus is!"

"For shame, brother, to speak so of the
good Santa Claus, who brings us such
beautiful gifts. I will watch for him, the
kind old Santa Claus, to come from the
gift land for us in all the wind and snow,"
and the little girl ran to the window and
drew aside the rich, heavy curtain.

"But Santa Claus always comes down the chimney, little Miss Wisdom," said the boy, joining her. "How it snows! I'm so glad. 'Twill be such fun for us boys to-morrow."

"'Tis the old woman up in the clouds, picking her goose for Christmas dinner," said the little girl, laughing and singing,—

"Old woman, up in the clouds so high,
   Making the feathers about us fly,
   Picking your goose for Christmas pie,
   Give me a piece of it by and by!"

Just then the mother was heard calling, and the children ran into the great parlor, all ablaze with light and beauty. In the center of all rose the beautiful Christmas tree, luminous with shining toys and many-hued candles.

Oh, it was delightful! To the little ones nothing could compare with the long-dreamed-of Christmas tree full of beautiful presents, just what they had been wanting, and hoped that wonderful old diviner, Santa Claus, would think of; and, of the whole year to them, no time was like the glorious Christmas season.

In quite another part of the town, very poor and squalid, lived the lace weavers.

In quaint old buildings, falling to ruins, they were huddled together, many wretched homes under one roof, yet even there they were trying to celebrate the birth of the blessed Christ child.

In the dingy rooms burned cheap tallow candles, and the little ones, with their poor wee gifts, were as happy as the brother and sister with the beautiful Christmas tree in the stately mansion.

One room only, a very small one, up in an attic in the lace-weavers' quarters, was in darkness. By the window stood a little, sorrowful girl, very pale-faced, all alone, watching the snow-flakes.

It was very cold, and her clothes were thin and ragged. She shivered, for she was quite chilled through. She was an orphan. The father had died, oh! long ago, one whole year, an age in the life of a child. Only the week before, the mother was driven away to her last home in the paupers' grave-yard, to rest in the plain deal coffin, till beautiful white wings should waft her up to Heaven the Golden.

It was very sad to see the little pale-faced child looking after the paupers' cart, driven so roughly over the frozen ground, and the kind-hearted neighbors had pitied her, and, though they were poor lace-makers like the mother, they had given her food with their sympathy, and promised to help her on with the trade.

They were true-hearted, honest folk, but

somehow in this joyous Christmas season
they had all forgotten her, and, far up in
the dreary attic-chamber of the old tene-
ment-house, she looked out into the night
and storm alone.

It was so dark in the room that she
could not bear to leave the window, though
the wind whistled in at the loose casement,
making quite a clatter, and causing her
little teeth to chatter with cold.

She was very hungry. She had eaten
the last crust the night before, and everybody had been so busy. It was not strange,
she thought, that they had forgotten her.

She could remember the last Christmas
they were all together. How busy the
mother was making the Christmas pie,
and how the father brought home a wood-
en doll, saying, "'T is for my good little
daughter," and kissed her. Then, taking
her on his shoulder, he danced all about

the room, and how the dear mother laughed.

She was so happy then, and now so desolate and wretched. Everybody else was happy; she heard the children shouting, and she was so faint and hungry.

Just then a man, in an oil-cloth coat and cap, came along, and lighted the street lamp opposite the window. That made it more cheerful; still, the child was so cold and hungry, she could bear it no longer.

"I will go out," she thought, "into the light. Perhaps I shall dare to go in somewhere. The neighbors have been so kind to me, but I'm not used to them as I was to the dear mother. I will wish them a 'Merry Christmas,' and they will give me something to eat. Then, perhaps, I can sleep, and go away in my dreams to the beautiful land where it is warm with God's pleasant sunshine."

Taking from the shelf a faded shawl and torn bonnet, which had been the mother's, she fastened them on as well as she could. But they were too large; it was all of no use, they would slip off again.

As she opened the door of her chamber, a great draught of wind rushed in from the street. Some one was coming in at the common staircase. She heard merry voices and footsteps on the stairs. She drew back into the darkness of her own room with shrinking timidity.

Very strange it was to her the cheery laughing, yet she had been as light-hearted once, but it seemed a great while ago.

When the sound of voices died away, she stole softly down the stairs to the door of the great front room, which had always been the grand place to her. Of all the neighbors, the woman in this best room had been most kind to her and the poor mother in *her* sickness.

The little cold fingers gave a timid knock, but, within, the father and mother were talking, and the little ones laughing so loud, that no one said the welcome " Come in," or came to open the door.

The cold winds whistled through the uncovered halls of the tenement house, and the child stood waiting with chattering teeth, and feet and hands so benumbed that she thought it would be better out in the street. There she could run and warm herself.

It was snowing fast, and the feathery flakes fell all over the worn shawl, covering its faded colors with soft white down; over the great bonnet that would fall back upon her neck; and over the rich, golden-brown curls, that were left bare to the storm.

As she ran on, the streets grew lighter, and on each side of the way were gay shops, with great windows filled with a thousand beautiful things. How much better it was than staying in the dark attic-room alone; and she thought, if she were not so cold and hungry, she could have quite enjoyed it.

There was a great jolly man walking on before her, humming a song. Presently he stopped to look in at a shop window, and she read in his broad, pleasant face that his heart was kind and loving. So, without stopping to dread it, she ran up to him, saying, "Please, sir, I wish you a merry Christmas."

"Ah, ha! little one," he said kindly, "you've caught a Christmas gift, but it is too stormy a night for little things like you to be out." Drawing from his pocket one of many small packages, he said, "My babies will never miss this. Now run home, like a good child; no doubt the mother is calling you now."

Then he hurried on, and the child, with trembling fingers, untied the parcel. How she hoped it was a piece of bread; but no! It was a pretty toy lamb, with a fleece as white as the snow that was covering her.

She was so much disappointed that the tears ran down her face very fast, and in the storm and cold this was uncomfortable.

Just then the beautiful chimes sounded from the great belfry of Bruges. This Christmas Eve they were played by a famous musician, who sat in the chamber below the belfry, and struck upon an immense key-board like that of a piano. These keys connect with hammers that strike the bells, so that in all the world

there are no chimes like those of the belfry
of Bruges.

There the grand musician sat and played,
throwing the whole harmony of his soul
into the music, and all the town of Bruges
stopped to listen, and, clasping each other's
hands, whispered softly, " How beautiful!"
for the divine music thrilled them.

Above all, it went to the heart of the
little hungry child, out alone in the pitiless
night and storm. The voices of the matchless chimes led her, and she hurried on to
the great belfry, clasping the pretty white
lamb closely in her little chilled hand.

Somehow she did not feel so hungry
now, and that was a blessing. There was
the stately mansion all ablaze with light.
She could look in through the rich crimson curtains of the grand parlor window,
and see the beautiful Christmas tree, and
the happy children dancing around it.

It was very near the belfry, and she sat down on the broad steps, and, wrapping her shawl about her, listened to the wonderful chimes.

Still the snow fell heavily, covering her over with its cold white mantle, but she did not move. The voice of the chimes was whispering in her ear such beautiful things. It was delightful, and all the dread shadows that filled the night and storm faded away, for they were only born of earth.

Yes! it told her of a great Christmas tree up in Heaven the Golden. There was a pure white robe and shining wings, the priceless gift of the Father's love. These were all marked with her name, and she was very happy.

She was no longer hungry nor cold, for the snow mantle was thick now over her little shrunken form. Only the tiny pale

face looked out from the white covering,
and that was leaning against the pillar
of the great doorway. The old bonnet
had fallen off, and she tried no longer
to confine it. When the storm was over
and the moon came out, it shone upon her
golden brown hair, making it luminous
with beauty.

How smoothly it sailed along, that crescent boat of the sky; and the deep blue
eyes watching it saw such marvelous sights
so pleasant, that a sweet peace gathered
around the child. The poor little heart,
that in the early hours of the blessed
Christmas Eve beat with the quick flutter
of fearful timidity and loneliness, was at
rest in the holy calm.

Yes! there was the dear mother in the
Golden Boat, so peaceful and free from
care. How tenderly her dear eyes shone,
and how beautiful she was in the radiant

light of heaven! She beckoned with her hand, and the little child reached eagerly out to her, crying, " It is the mother! Oh, mother, dear, I am coming! Wait, mother! I am com—"

Up to the Crescent Boat on to Heaven the Golden, and to the throne of the loving God, had passed the spirit of the little child. Just then a bright star fell down from the fleecy clouds and rested upon the pure, ice-cold forehead, leaning so heavily against the great pillar of the stately doorway.

The cadence of the last chime was dying away upon the still night air. It was twelve o'clock, and the musician went home. The great belfry was left silent, and in the coming of the holy Christmas dawning all the peaceful town of Bruges slept.

In the morning the servant found a little child dead upon the door steps of the

grand mansion, with the frost glittering
like a crown of glory in her golden hair.
It was said she was a poor lace-maker's
child, who had died in great poverty and
want. The crowd gathered about the door,
saying, "It is sad, oh! very sad!" but they
knew nothing of what the music of the
bells had been to her—nothing of the
Golden Boat.

At last, when men came to take the
poor little thing away to the paupers'
burying-ground, the good mother of the
house said, "No, do not take her away,
I entreat you."

Then she folded the child in her arms,
kissing her pale cheeks and golden hair,
saying, "I will see to it. The good Lord
led her to my door, and, though it is late,
I will do all there is left me. She shall
rest in the pleasant garden under the lin-
den-trees."

Dear little one! We can do nothing more now, but in Heaven the Golden the loving God will receive her, a most precious Christmas offering!

GOLDEN SNOW.

THE snow-flakes were falling all over the northern Gold Land, for it was mid-winter. Against the ice-bound shore the angry breakers of the great Pacific dashed, and the wind whistled like a trumpeter.

A warm fire burned on the hearth of the fisherman's hut, and with a red face the good-wife bent over it, preparing the supper. The old man stood by the window looking out, and thinking his poor thoughts of the wind and the tide, which ended always with the same refrain, "God help us fisher folk!" Suddenly he gave a quick start, exclaiming—" Hark! wife; what is that?"

The old woman dropped the wooden

spoon, and listened to the clear voices that
rose above the storm:—

> " Golden Snow! Golden Snow!
> To and fro;
> Over her little heart
> We blow,
> Our dear little sister,
> Golden Snow.

> " Open your door,
> That the fire-light's glow
> May tinge the cheek
> Of Golden Snow —
> Oh! dear little sister,
> Golden Snow."

Then came the savage old trumpeter,
and blew a great blast close by the door
and window of the little hut. It was
really quite startling, and the old woman
clung to her husband's arm; but above
all they could hear the shrill clear voices
calling—

> " Open the door,
> For the wild winds blow
> Over the heart
> Of Golden Snow."

"I can not do it," said the good-wife, trembling; but the old man walked straight to the door. Though his wife entreated him, saying, "It is the Evil One who calls without, dear husband, do not open it," he lifted the latch fearlessly. With a great bang in rushed the wind and blew out the candle.

"God save us!" cried the good-wife, crossing herself, almost ready to swoon with fright.

A bright glow from the fire fell upon a willow basket, covered with a fine crimson cloth. As the old man took it up, a little wailing cry rose, which touched the woman's heart more than all her fears. Taking it from her husband, she exclaimed—

"God pity it! It is a little innocent child!"

The old man pressed hard upon the door, and drove out the ugly wind. Then

he came to the fire, and saw his wife folding in her kind arms the most beautiful
little child that even a poet could imagine.
She was as white as a snow-flake, only the
rose tinge upon her cheeks and her lips
were like ripe cherries. Her hair was soft
as silk, and lay in pretty waves of gold
about her head, like the shining crown of
a little princess.

The good people were greatly bewildered; but when they looked into the
liquid blue eyes of the little one, it seemed
like a deep fountain of happiness that was
opened to them, and they were delighted
beyond measure. As they had no children,
this child seemed like a God's gift, and
they adopted her for their own.

Her little robes were of the finest mate-
rial, daintily embroidered, but among them
all there was nothing to tell her name or
parentage, only a coral necklace with a

golden clasp, engraved with the letters
" G. S."

" Was ever any thing so strange?" said
the good-wife. " But she is our child now,
and we will call her Golden Snow, for her
hair is shining like gold, and her complexion fair as the driven snow."

The poor fisher-folk had now something
to love, and were never so happy in their
lives.

The long winter gave place to the pleasant summer time, and the little child grew
lovelier day by day, till in all the northern
gold land there was not a maiden who
could compare with her.

Good fortune had followed the fisherman. Ever since that stormy night he
had never drawn in his net empty, and
there had been always plenty in the larder.
The old woman often said, " It all comes
of Golden Snow—she is our luck child."

As the years went by, she had taught
the maiden all she knew herself, which was
little enough, to be sure; but the child
had other teachers. From the birds she
received the gift of song, and learned the
wonderful stories of the far southern lands.

The leaves of summer, and the ever-
greens of winter, whispered a thousand
pleasant things in her ear, but it was the
snow-flakes that she loved best of all. The
old fisher-folk often heard them calling her
as they flew about in the winter storm:—

> "Golden Snow! Golden Snow!
>   You are one of us.
>   When the wild winds blow,
>   Come out to us
>   From the firelight's glow.
>   You are our sister,
>   Golden Snow."

Then, before the good-wife could stop
her, the little maiden would fly out into
the storm, full of joy, dancing about as
lightly as the snow-flakes themselves.

At first the old fisherman would run
after her, and bring her in quickly, for
fear that the chill of the storm would kill
her; but when he saw that this only saddened her, and how rosy, laughing, and
healthful she always was with the snow-
flakes, he said to the good-wife—

"They do not harm her—let the child
have her way."

After this they would stand by the window watching her; and very often they
heard her saying—

"My pretty sisters, how merry we are—
how much I love you! The winter, oh!
the winter, is the joy time, and my sisters
the fairies of the winter."

Then the snow-flakes would answer:—

> "Golden Snow.
> Many maids are fair,
>   We know,
> But none like the princess
> Golden Snow."

2*

So it happened that the old fisher-folk
found out that Golden Snow was a princess, and they no longer wondered at the
innate grace of the lovely child. Every
thing she said, and all her ways, was so
charming that it was impossible to resist
her; but as she was so gentle and good,
this was all well. Every night, before she
went to sleep, she said reverently—" Our
Father, who art in heaven." The loving
God heard her, and kept her heart pure,
as she passed on through the portals of
childhood into timid, dreamy maidenhood.

One day, in the winter time, when Golden
Snow was about fifteen years old, a herald
rode by the fisherman's cottage, crying—
" The prince! the prince will marry the
most beautiful maiden in all the Gold
Land. Hear! hear! the prince will marry
the most beautiful maiden in all the Gold
Land!"

Then the old fisherman went out and asked the messenger what it meant.

"It means this," replied the man, "that though the prince and all his ancestors were born in Russia, he has determined to marry only in the Gold Land, and the most beautiful maiden. For you must know, that though he is so high born in the old world, the estates are getting poor, but here he has won every thing. He has opened a mine so rich that he will never be able to count his money. He wishes his children to be real lords of the Gold Land—to be miner princes. So here he will marry even the poorest maiden, but she must be the most beautiful."

Then he told how all the lovely young girls in the country were invited to a great feast at the castle, and that the prince would choose a wife from among them.

After this, the herald went crying before

every house, no matter how humble, for
this was the command of the prince.

The old fisherman went into the cottage,
and told all to the good-wife.

" Golden Snow is the most beautiful
maiden," she answered.

" Yes," said the old man, " Golden Snow
is the most beautiful, but he who wins
must seek her. She should not go to the
castle for a husband, even though he were
a king."

This grieved the mother, for all her life
she had eaten the bread of toil, and she
longed to see the dainty fingers of her
adopted child covered with rings, and to
have her wear costly trailing robes, such
as the wives and daughters of the great
miner princes wore.

In the corner sat Golden Snow, braid-
ing her silken hair, which was so long it
swept the ground. She bound the broad

plaits about her head, and formed a shiny crown.

" Was there ever any thing like it ?" said the old woman, sighing, and passing her brown hand fondly over the beautiful tresses.

" The father is right," replied Golden Snow. " My sisters will see to it. Have never a care, mother;" and the maiden began singing the nightingale's song, till the rafters of the old hut rang with the silvery melody.

" The chit of a child has never a care," thought the old woman, " but it is different with me, who know what life is."

All through the north land there was great excitement. Everywhere the young girls wrought upon gay dresses, and the fathers and mothers consulted together, that nothing might be wanting in the ball costumes of their daughters, for each one thought—"Our child is the most beautiful maiden."

The morning dawned without a ray of sunshine. Only the heavy snow-clouds covered the sky.

"My sisters are getting ready for the ball to-night," laughed Golden Snow. "Very soon the messengers will be flying out after the fleecy fringes and ribbons, for every one must be dressed in the real court costume."

"Silly child, silly child," answered the old woman; yet silently she thought—"If my daughter could go to the ball, the prince would surely fall in love with her, for in all the north land she is the only true princess."

"See, they are coming, mother!" exclaimed Golden Snow, clapping her hands with delight.

The old woman looked out of the win-

dow, and saw everywhere the snow-flakes
flying about, like little madcaps, over hill
and valley.

It seemed a long day to her; there was
a chill in the air, and she was not happy.
Satos, the old fisherman, came in, saying,
in his good-natured voice, " It will be
stormy to-night, wife."

" Ah, well," replied she, " what will that
matter to us, who stay at home?"

Just then a knock came at the door;
and when the old man opened it, he saw a
stately lady, who was so covered with
snow that no part of her dress could be
seen. It was like a cloak about her. Upon
her head she wore a band of shining brilliants, that so dazzled the old man that he
could not speak a word.

The lady stepped into the cottage, and
when she saw Golden Snow, she embraced
her fondly, saying, " My dear child, I have

not forgotten that it is your birthday, and that you are now fifteen years old." She took a little box from her pocket, and placed it upon the floor. In a few moments it had increased to so great a size that it was large enough to hold the entire wardrobe of a lady.

Golden Snow kissed her hand, and thanked her again and again.

" I must go now," said the lady; " I can not endure the heat; but never fear, my child, for your sisters shall attend to every thing. Now, good-bye;" and again she embraced the young maiden tenderly, and in a moment was gone.

The fisherman and his wife had been standing gazing upon this scene in silent amazement; but when the lady had disappeared, and they could not see how, the old woman recovered her voice—

" Father," she exclaimed, " the lady! she

did not go out at the door, nor the window; how did she go?"

"Don't ask me, wife—I don't know anything," replied the old man in a bewildered way. "I believe—I rather think I am in the fog." And after this he sank into a chair, and did not speak again for an hour. He was trying in vain to get out of the fog. A clear, ringing laugh startled the old man; it was Golden Snow, whose eyes were glistening with mirth.

"Who was she, child?" asked the goodwife.

"It was the Snow Queen, mother," replied the young girl, as soon as she could speak for laughing. "But now let us look at my birthday gift."

The good woman's curiosity overcame her wonder; so, taking the silver key, she unlocked the great box, and displayed such a quantity of beautiful things, that

her admiration was as great as her amazement.

There were shining robes of silver and
gold cloth, and rich cloaks of fur, ornamented with glittering gems. Golden Snow
was almost wild with delight, and her
beaming eyes glistened with the unexpect-
ed pleasure. And the good-wife, though
the mysticism troubled her greatly, could
not but rejoice at the sight of all these
treasures.

She took up a robe of silver cloth, richly
embroidered with gold, saying, "Oh! my
child, if you could only wear this to the
ball, I should live to see you the bride of a
real prince, and the richest man in all the
Russian possessions, except the great czar
himself."

The old woman sighed heavily, adding,
" It would not be right to say aught against
the good-man, for there is nobody like

him; but I do believe he would have his way if old Nickey Bend stood at the door with his cloven hoof, so it is no use talking—we must give up the ball, my child."

"And I am content," said Golden Snow, fastening a string of pearls into the shining crown that she had formed of her own abundant tresses. Then she threw about her a rich fur mantle, made of a thousand different skins of the finest quality.

"I must go now, and dance for a while with my sisters. Remember, mother," she added, as the old woman shook her head, "it is my birthnight—you would not deny me."

The old woman listened, and heard the clear voices calling:—

> " 'Tis thy birthnight, sister fair,
>   Join us fairies of the air.
>   Where the night-winds round us blow
>   We are waiting, Golden Snow."

"Kiss me, mother, for I must go," said the maiden, eagerly. And with the old woman's kiss warm upon her cheek, she ran out and danced with the pretty snow-flakes till her face glowed and her eyes sparkled like the rich carbuncle that clasped her mantle.

"It is getting late; come in, child! come in!" called the old woman, who grew weary waiting.

The maiden kissed her white hands to the fleecy snow-flakes, singing like a bird—

> " Good night!
> Snow-flakes white,
> Golden Snow
> Now must go.
> Sisters white,
> Good night! Good night!"

There was a little sound, as though soft hands met and young lips kissed each other, and Golden Snow ran into the house, rosy, joyous, and ready to obey the good mother, even when she said, " Go to bed, my dear child," though the bright eyes were still wide awake.

" You will tell me a story, mother," said the young girl, in a coaxing tone.

So the old woman sat down by the bed-side, and told her a wonderful story of the olden time, how a fair princess was changed into a blue bird by the incantations of a wicked old witch, who had red eyes, and had studied the black art. And how, after a long time, the cruel enchantment was broken by a brave young prince, who had marvelous adventures. " So it all ended happily," said the old mother, bending over Golden Snow to kiss her. Then she saw that the young maiden slept, and she stood gazing upon her fresh young face, and thinking curious thoughts, which somehow were enwoven with the web of the story she had been telling, but all ended in

this:—" Golden Snow is the most beautiful maiden."

*   *   *   *   *   *

At the castle the musicians were playing, and the grand saloon was like an
enchanted hall, with fragrant air and gor-
geous light. The delicious music stole into
the heart, and throbbed in the impassioned
pulses of the guests, the noble gentlemen
and fair ladies.

The dark-eyed brunette rivaled the delicate blonde, and all were lovely in their
dainty robes, with the soft mellow light
floating around them

Amid the festive throng, with courtly
hospitality, walked the young prince. The
winds and sun had bronzed his handsome
face, and the damp exhalations of the mine
had moistened the rich curls of his dark
hair. Yet nothing in all the rough miner's

life had harmed him in any way. He was
a prince born, and a real prince at heart.
There was not a father in the north land
who would not have taken him by the
hand, nor a mother who would not have
been proud of him. Even the young maidens whispered together, "He is a *man;*
one could look up to him, and that is the
best of all."

The prince was attentive to all his fair
guests, but he danced more with the consul's daughter. She was a proud young
beauty, so ambitious, that she had treated
with scorn many an honest heart in the
Gold Land.

"My great-great-grandfather was younger
brother to an earl, and I am beautiful
enough to be the bride of a noble-
man," she would say, as she sat by her
mirror. When the herald came with
the invitation to the ball, she determined

in her mind to marry the rich Russian prince.

"Of course," she thought, "I am the most beautiful, so that is settled. I will go back to the old world, where I will astonish even the queen with the richness of my dress and the luster of my jewels, and every one will pay court to the princess of the Gold Land."

So she went to the ball with glistening eyes and a proud flush upon her cheek, and all the guests whispered, "The consul's daughter is the most beautiful maiden." It found an echo in the heart of the prince, so that the matter seemed really decided.

Just then the music ceased, for the musicians were weary. The dancers were quite out of breath, and the windows of the grand saloon were opened to admit the refreshing air.

Without, the snow-flakes were holding their revel in honor of the princess Golden Snow. Up to the great carved windows they flew, and their clear voices sounded through the ball-room so distinctly, that the prince and all his guests heard them:

> " The consul's daughter is fair, we know,
> But not like the beautiful Golden Snow.
> There are lovely maids at the castle ball,
> But Golden Snow is fairer than all."

The flush of pride in the cheek of the consul's daughter gave place to the deeper red of anger. Her eyes shot flames of fire, and her brow darkened with heavy clouds. "What does this insult mean?" she said sharply to the prince.

The young man gave a start, as though he were awaking from a dream. "It is strange," he answered, "but it shall be looked to, lady. What it means I can not tell."

3

He called his servants, telling them to bring in the people who were crying without. When the men returned, they were trembling, and seemed quite afraid.

"There are a hundred voices, but no person is without, only the snow-flakes flying about like living things."

Then the prince went out himself, and a great search was made all over the grounds of the castle, but not a human being could be found. Still, everywhere the voices could be heard, and the snow-flakes thickened, till at last the search was given up.

"It is the work of magic and evil," said the consul and all his friends; but the prince offered a great reward to any one who would find the beautiful Golden Snow, and all the guests were invited to return in one week's time.

All the week the young prince could think of nothing but the mysterious voices that pursued him, and everywhere his messengers were seeking for the beautiful Golden Snow.

The consul's daughter was nearly wild with rage and disappointment. One evening, in the dusky twilight, she went down into the shadows of a dark cañon, and consulted a wicked old witch, who lived in a dismal cavern.

"Am I not the fairest of all the maidens in the new world?" she asked, "but what means this cry of 'Golden Snow?'"

"You are very fair," answered the old witch, "but I must read the stars." So she went down into the lowest depths of the cañon, and in the bottom of a deep well she read the stars:—

"There were maidens fair at the prince's ball,
But Golden Snow is fairer than all."

"What does it mean?" asked the consul's daughter, pale and trembling with emotion.

"I will tell you! Golden Snow is the Elixir of Beauty, and if you can obtain it, and wash in it, you will become the most enchanting maiden in the world."

"Where shall I find it? I will give you any thing—any thing for this Elixir of Beauty."

Then the witch told her, if she would promise to be her slave one day in every month, she would help her to procure the great treasure.

"I can buy the old woman off when I become the bride of the rich prince," thought the young girl. So she promised, and the witch brought out a wrinkled yellow parchment, and wrote the contract. Piercing the maiden's arm, she dipped the pen in the blood, and the consul's daughter signed it with a trembling hand.

"That is good," said the old witch, her red eyes glaring at the maiden. "Now you must go to the summit of the black mountain, just over the prince's mine, and bring me a quart of the snow that has drifted round the roots of the blasted pine. All your gold and jewelry you must bring, and, at twelve o'clock to-morrow night, come to the cavern, and I will give you the Elixir of Beauty, the wonderful golden snow."

The consul's daughter took off all her jewelry, necklace, bracelets, and all the gold she had she gave to the old witch. Then she toiled up the steep mountain, and at last, weary and worn, returned with the snow from the roots of the blasted pine.

When the young girl had left the cavern, the woman bent over the blazing fire, with alembic and crucible. "Who can tell the

wonderful mystery," she muttered to herself, as the liquid boiled up yellow as gold.
"I myself will wash in it, and become young and fair again."

The night came on in darkness, and at eleven o'clock the old witch carried the liquid out in the chill air, and with her red eyes, that could see best in the darkness, watched it as it changed in form, till, just as the bell in the church tower rung out twelve, she saw before her the Elixir of Beauty, the magic golden snow.

Just at that moment she heard the voice of the consul's daughter calling, "It is so dark, I cannot see; give me your hand, and lead me to the Elixir of Beauty. I have dared so much for it! I am almost dead with fright."

"In a moment," answered the old woman, and she slipped the golden snow into a crevice in the rock, leaving only a little for the maiden. Reaching out her hand, she led the trembling girl into the cavern, and, taking an ivory box, filled it with pure white snow. Sprinkling over it the remnant of the Elixir of Beauty, she gave it to the maiden, saying, "Wash in it, and you will become as lovely as the dawn."

When the young girl opened the box, it looked to her yellow and shiny, for the old witch had cast a glamour over it, so she went away quite satisfied.

She concealed her treasure in her private closet, and every night, after all in the house had retired, she washed her face, and, because there was the remnant of the Elixir of Beauty in it, she became fairer every day. All who saw her wondered, and said, "Surely the consul's daughter is the most beautiful maiden!"

Through the whole week the herald of the prince rode over the Gold Land, everywhere seeking for Golden Snow. Once he passed the fisherman's cottage, but that morning the fisher folk and their adopted child had gone down to the beach. As chance would have it, they missed the messenger.

Again the castle was illuminated, and the guests were assembled.

There were beautiful maidens, but the consul's daughter shone like the morning. Again the heart of the prince re-echoed the wondering admiration of the guests, and his deep dark eyes flashed with a strange magnetic fire.

As the evening advanced, it grew warm, with the great lights flashing everywhere, and the delicious notes of the music vibrating and thrilling in every form.

" Do not open the windows," entreated the consul's daughter, " for the snow-flakes are drifting with the wind, and the night

air is chill." A shudder passed over her,
so they opened only the doors of the grand
saloon. But one of the warm and weary
dancers went out secretly, and opened the
carved oval window of the great hall.
Then, louder than ever, the clear voices
floated into the hall, and in all the winding
corridors found a hundred echoes, till the
whole castle reverberated with them :—

> " The consul's daughter is fair, we know,
> But not like the princess Golden Snow.
> There are lovely maids at the castle ball,
> But Golden Snow is fairer than all."

The consul's daughter was again frantic
with rage; her eyes glared with fury, and
her face grew frightful with the heat of
passion. The dream had passed forever
from the heart of the prince, and he wondered that, only a moment before, he had
thought the face, so contorted with anger,
beautiful as a painter's bright ideal.

3*

Everywhere they searched, but could find no one, so, while the mystery deepened, the ball ended.

In the morning, the prince mounted a fine black horse, and started off as for a long journey. For months he wandered over the northern Gold Land, seeking everywhere the princess Golden Snow.

At last, when he had given up all hope, and was returning disappointed to the castle, he chanced to ride by the fisherman's cottage. The old fisher folk sat in the corner mending a net, and Golden Snow, in her rich, marvelous voice, was singing to them one of the songs of the sea. The prince stopped his horse and listened, drinking in every note of the delicious melody. When it was ended, he dismounted, and, leading his horse by the bridle, knocked at the door, and the goodwife opened it.

"Tell me, good mother, who it was singing, for, in all my life, never a voice came so into my heart."

"It was the princess Golden Snow," answered the old woman, proudly.

The prince entered, and saw Golden Snow in all her matchless grace and beauty. Around her head was her crown of shining hair, decked with brilliants, and a mantle of the richest fur covered her. She had only just returned from the sea-shore, with the rich flush of exercise upon her cheek, and her eyes were beaming with the rare beauty of her gentle spirit.

The fisherman rose to meet the young prince, who told him, in his handsome, manly way, how all over the north land he had been seeking for the princess Golden Snow; and how at last, when hope was almost dying, he had found the treasure.

The old man listened gravely; then he placed the white hand of the maiden in the young man's strong, true palm, saying, " Not because you are a Russian prince, but because you are one of God's noblemen, I give you my dear child. Take her, for in her loving heart she is the most beautiful maiden."

Thus the young people were betrothed in the cottage of the good fisher folk, and, when the news spread over the country, there was great rejoicing. They were married at the old church, where the stones are covered with lichens, and many a poor man's heart was made glad by the generosity of the prince that day.

The consul's daughter was too angry to join in the festivities, but all the former guests of the castle were there, and among them sat the fisher folk in the place of honor.

All over the northern Gold Land flew the joyous snow-flakes, dancing at the wedding of their princess.

Everywhere in the grand saloon, and through the winding corridors of the castle, with strains of rich music mingled the clear mysterious voices:—

> " All the north land now shall know,
> The most beautiful maiden is Golden Snow.
> We are her sisters, snow-flakes white,
> She is the princess of golden light."

Thus all were happy, save the consul's daughter, whose pride and rage devoured her. For one day every month she was doomed to be the slave of the wicked old witch, which was wretchedness. At last, one night, when her tasks had been too hard for endurance, from her great weariness and sickness of heart, she cried out, " O Lord Christ, forgive and pity me!"

Then the old witch gave a wild shriek

of madness, and disappeared in the black
shadows of the cañon forever.

Because she had hidden part of the
golden snow, by this prayer the maiden
was delivered out of her hands.

The selfish pride of the consul's daughter was humbled, and she grew so gentle
and good, that all, even the poor and de-
pendent, learned to love her, so that she,
too, became, in heart, a beautiful maiden.

GRACIA AND CATRINA.

NEAR the Mission of San Diego lived a very wealthy Spaniard and his wife, the most beautiful señora in all the country for many miles around.

They had every thing about them to make life pleasant: a fine orange and lemon grove; a large garden, containing olive, almond, peach, and pear trees; indeed, all kinds of fruit and flowers, that the luxurious climate of San Diego produces.

Their house was pleasant, and furnished with all the comforts and many of the luxuries of life; and when God blessed them with a little daughter, they felt as though there was nothing left to wish for. The child resembled her beautiful mamma

in features as much as the tiny bud is like
the full-blown rose.

The hidalgo had never ceased to regard
his wife with that kind of worshipful love
so dear to woman's heart; and his great
delight was to watch tenderly over mother
and child, that even the slightest wish
might not pass ungratified.

As it grew older, the little one learned
to recognize the glance of love; and when
at last it would open its large dark eyes
and look eagerly at the dear papa, and,
holding out its tiny hands, crow with all
the innocent delight of infancy, he would
take the babe in his arms, and all the
harsh lines about his mouth softened into
smiles. He was happier than any one in
the whole country, except the delighted
mother, who was never weary of looking
upon the darling of her heart.

The señora was a devout Catholic, and,

Gracia and Catrina.

though she seldom left the child alone
with her nurse, as the feast of Corpus
Christi approached, she felt that this year,
above all others so blessed to her in the
birth of her beloved child, she should
assist in the celebration. On the morning
of the holy day, she gave her treasure,
with many charges, into the care of the
old servant, bidding her on no account
whatever to leave the child, even for a
moment. Twice, as she was about leaving,
she returned to embrace the little one,
with her soft eyes filled with tears. As
she covered the face of her babe with
kisses, she whispered, " Mamma loves thee.
Mijita mia. Foolish mamma trembles to
leave thee, yet the divine eye of the Holy
Mother will watch over thee. *Mia vida,
mia vida!*" Then came the sound of music, and the voice of the hidalgo calling
her; so with a last embrace, with mingled

smiles and tears, the young mother parted from her little one, for the first time since its birth.

There was to be a large procession formed upon the plaza, where rustic booths were built, and ornamented according to the taste and wealth of the devout, who often sacrificed the comfort of weeks, to be able to give this tribute of honor to the Holy Mother and the Blessed Christ.

Pictures of the Madonna were placed upon the rude altars, entwined with beautiful wreaths, while rare flowers shed their rich incense from costly vases. The señora had spared neither money nor pains.

"It is in honor of the Merciful Christ— the Redeemer of the world," she said; "let every thing be as worthy of His greatness as possible; it will fall far short of what my thankful heart would offer."

Pictures from the hands of the old mas-

ters were brought from the house, with
tapestry and fringes; and every thing that
the luxurious climate produced was added,
until nothing seemed wanting to make it
the one booth of enchanting beauty.

The señora superintended the arrange-
ment of all, while the señor sat a little
apart, watching with delight the magic
workings of her exquisite taste and refine-
ment. All this time the nurse held the
infant in her arms, singing quaint old
Indian ballads, rocking her to and fro
with a soothing motion, till at last the
restless fingers were stilled and the pretty
eyes closed. The little one slept, and
dreamed, no doubt, such dreams as the
loving God sends to guileless infancy.

Just then the procession started, and
the music fell upon the ear of the young
Indian girl who was always near to wait
upon old Macata, the nurse.

"Macata," she said, as she started lightly from the mat on which she was sitting, " it touches my heart; I must go! See, the baby sleeps. Nothing can harm it. Come, mother Macata, only for a moment!"

"Nothing can harm it," said the old Indian, as she laid the child in its little straw cradle, for she, too, loved the festive sight and glad music of the *fête*.

She had wished, of all things, to join the gossips of the mission on the plaza, but, since that could not be, she saw no reason, while the child was sleeping so sweetly, that she should not go to the garden wall, and for a few moments catch a passing glimpse of the gay procession. She bent over the child, patting it softly with her great strong hand, and singing in a low voice:—

> " Sleep! baby, sleep!
> While I softly creep

To the roadside near;
Sleep, baby, dear."

The little form was so still and peaceful. Surely there could be no danger! So the nurse, who loved her dearly, knelt down and kissed her very lightly, saying, in the Indian tongue,

" Master of life, preserve the little white rosebud."

Again she pressed her dusky lips to the sweet little face, so peaceful in its innocent repose, then ran away through the garden to the roadside, with her companion, the bright-eyed Indian girl.

It was a rare sight in the eyes of these simple Indians, that long procession, with its swelling music and waving banners. All the Indian lads and maidens in the country were there, dressed in their gala attire, while the bright-colored handkerchiefs and shawls of the more rustic señoras, as they rode by on horseback, added not a little to the festive scene.

For full fifteen minutes they sat watching the procession, crouching behind the garden wall, that the señora might not see them. Well they knew her eyes would be attracted by the magnetism of love to her child and home.

"See, mother Macata," said the young girl, sorrowfully, "there are all my mates, while I am here. Oh! how I wish I could go with them!"

Just then the señora passed, and, mid all the joy of the occasion, Macata saw a look of deep solicitude in her face as she turned toward the house. "We must go," said the old woman, taking the hand of the young girl.

"Only one moment," replied the maiden; and while old Macata yielded, she could not suppress an emotion of uneasiness which the señora's look had nervously roused.

"Now! now!" said the old woman, nervously, as again she clasped the hand of the girl, and dragged her away from the attractive scene.

"You know the baby sleeps," said the girl, pettishly; but Macata, in her uneasiness, hurried onward.

They passed through the pleasant garden into the silent house, and the softly shaded room where they had left the sleeping child. There stood the dainty little cradle, but the child was gone!

At first they thought some of the servants had returned and taken it to some other room; but when they had searched the whole house, and ran, calling in vain, through the garden, they were almost wild with fright.

Tears streamed from the eyes of the

young girl as she looked helplessly into
the face of old Macata, who tore her long
hair, and moaned piteously. She could
not cease looking, although it seemed
hopeless.

"In so short a time to disappear, and
leave no trace behind to aid this search!"
The child! The poor little innocent child
she loved so dearly, gone, she knew not
where! How could she meet the father
and mother?

Thus, full of despair, she ran about,
looking in vain, and calling wildly upon
her darling, until the señor and his wife
returned.

To picture the scene that followed would
be impossible. The torturing grief of the
unhappy father was mingled with all the
terrors of suspense, and the desolate heart
of the sorrowing mother refused to be
comforted. Day and night she sobbed

bitterly, "Would that God had taken my baby to himself!"

The whole country was roused. The search continued for many days, till hope died out in every heart. Then it was that a fearful fever seized the mother, exhausted by grief, want of sleep, and the fatigues of a hopeless search. For weeks her life was despaired of; and when at last the fever left her, the light had gone from her eye, the smile from her lips, and the hope of happiness from her heart.

The old Macata never left her side. At first the mother shuddered when she came near; but as she looked upon the hair of the old woman, which, since the loss of the child, had become white as the driven snow, her heart softened, and she shed her first tears upon the bosom of the penitent and sorrowing nurse.

For many weeks the luxury of tears had

4

been denied her, and, from that first bursting of the flood-gates of her grief, she could not bear the old Indian long out of her sight. A mutual sorrow bound their hearts together.

Macata could never do enough for the dear, sad señora, but sometimes she would go to her, saying, "Bless me now, señora dear; I am going to look for our baby."

Then the señora would bless her, and say, "Go, my poor Macata."

All day long she roamed through woods, down deep into the shadowy cañons, or upon the mountain tops. After weary hours, and sometimes days, of fruitless search, she would return, worn and heart-broken with her vain wanderings. Kneeling before the señora, weeping, and wringing her hands, she would cry, "Oh! dear señora, forgive me! I have not found our baby. I lost it, but I will find it. I will find it before I die, so help me, Wacondah, Great Spirit!"

Often the old woman fell fainting at the feet of her beloved señora, who would have her raised tenderly and placed upon the bed, where for hours she sat by her, watching and weeping.

Thus these two sorrowing ones, the broken-hearted mother and the grief-crazed nurse, became very dear to each other.

The father mourned deeply, but to the heart of man time brings its softening balm. He loved his wife fondly, and, for her sake, sometimes tried to waken a hope that the child might be restored to them. Yet within his shadowed heart he mourned the precious one as dead.

Very sadly he missed the tiny out-stretched hands that once were sure to greet him, and that radiant little face that was all the world to him; and as months and years went by, whenever he looked upon a little maiden full of grace and beauty, he would press his hand to his heart in sorrow, for "what might have been."

Sometimes the señora, leaning her weary head on his breast, would say: "I shall know my darling, no matter how many years shall pass before we meet." Then she would clasp her hands, exclaiming: "What if I should die before Macata finds her? Then, oh! then, I shall know her in heaven," she would bow her head lower upon the beloved breast in prayer. Thus she would remain till the tender voice of the hidalgo aroused her; then she would clasp her thin hands about his neck, and look pityingly into his eyes to see the sorrow of her heart reflected there.

Thus it was with the parents as the years passed sadly by, but all the while the seasons went and came again; the sunshine gladdened the earth; the rainbow beautified the **shower**; the flowers blossomed **in the** garden; and young hearts beat happily **as theirs upon their** bridal day.

\#   *   \#   *   *   \#   *

On that bright morning **of the** fête of **Corpus** Christi, which resulted **so** unfortunately for the hidalgo and the poor señora. Macata had not noticed that the garden gate was left unlocked, nor in her haste did **she see** the crouching **form of** a fierce-looking woman hiding behind the lime-tree.

No sooner was she and the young girl out of sight than the woman rose stealthily, and gathering up **her coarse** brown cloak around her, glided swiftly through the garden and **into** the room where the cradle stood, still moving from the parting motion of Macata's hand. Glancing hastily **around,** she snatched **up** the still sleeping

child, and wrapping it in the folds of her
cloak, ran out of the garden, away from the
road, on through the orange-grove, and before Macata and the girl returned, was far
away out of sight.

Still on she went, through the vineyard,
and over the hill beyond; nor did she
pause for a moment after she entered the
thick wood, until miles away in the dusk
of the evening, deep down in a cañon she
came to a rude cottage overhung with trees
and rocks.

All day long the delicate child had
been out in the burning sunshine, tast-
ing nothing but a tortilla moistened in
water.

When they entered the cottage she had
cried herself to sleep, and her little head
rested wearily upon the bosom of the
woman who had stolen her from her mother
and her happy home.

On the floor sat a little girl shelling beans. She was a poor, misshapen child of misfortune, with a sad mark of suffering upon her face, which, when the woman entered, deepened.

"Take this child, Catrina. Put it away anywhere—anywhere out of sight. It is hateful to me." Then throwing off the brown cloak, and rubbing her hands, she drew near the fire, adding: "Be in a hurry, girl. Give me my supper, for I am tired and hungry."

The young girl had taken the little one and laid it upon the bed, and, though there was an expression of surprise upon her face, she placed the supper upon the table without speaking. Then, placing chairs, she and the woman sat down together. Still not a word was spoken. By and by, after they had eaten, and the dishes were washed, the hearth swept, and more fagots heaped upon the fire, the girl pointed to the sleeping child.

"Let her be," said the woman, crossly. "I can not support you in idleness. Go shell your beans."

The girl placed a cup of milk at the fire, sat down again to her task, and, for a long time, nothing was heard but the crackling pods. At length the woman spoke.

"It is little use in talking to you, Catrina: but I must speak sometimes, and you are the only being I have about me, and you can not tell what I say. You can not remember, Catrina! Many years ago I was beautiful; I was young. Now I am old, not with years! See this hair once so glossy—look at it."

She caught out the comb with an angry grasp, and all over her neck and shoulders fell the heavy tangles of long, gray hair.

"I was young, beautiful, and beloved.

Oh, it seems an age of years ago! I have been so wretched since. That child's father caused his death! I lived! God knows how till your father came, and I married him. For love? Oh, no, for the poor protection that woman's nature craves and a shelter from despair. But even this failed me!

"What a life for both! But I am revenged, ha! ha! They will wait long for their pretty darling, now." The woman laughed wildly, and such a look of hate and exultation covered her face, that, in the fitful fire-light, was almost fiendish.

Catrina dropped her hands on her lap, and shuddered, while her eyes were fixed upon the wretched woman with a kind of fascination.

"Go to work! go to work! I say, you stupid little witch, what are you staring at? You look as if you were frightened out of the little sense you have."

4*

Again the woman laughed a strange laugh, that grated harshly upon the ear of the unfortunate girl. Tears filled her eyes, but still no reply.

Poor child! she had never spoken one word in her short but sorrowful life. She was only the poor little step-daughter of the woman, and since the death of her father she had been unhappy.

The noise had awakened the little one, and opening her large eyes, she looked around first with wonder, and then with fear, at the strange place and strange faces before her. The woman rose and took her in her arms.

"So, little chick, you are awake, and how do you think your lady mamma feels now, and your proud papa? Ha! ha! he never thought how I felt, when years ago he brought death to my heart, nor will I think of him."

Slowly she began swaying the child to and fro, talking fiercely all the while. The tiny lips of the baby quivered, as, for a moment, she suppressed her cry, then a pitiful wail filled the cottage.

Catrina was preparing the bowl of bread and milk, and as she approached, the little one held out her hands, and when Catrina took her she hid her face in her bosom and sobbed softly. The child was hungry, and as the girl offered her the bread and milk, she ate it eagerly, but all the while her frightened gaze was fixed upon the face of the woman, who seemed to grow uneasy before the pitiful terror of those innocent eyes.

"It is always so now. Even this child shrinks from me, and I don't mean to harm her. She has her bread and milk here, if it is not in a silver bowl. Ah! my heart is of stone, now—of stone!" and instinctively she folded her arms over her bosom, and, rocking herself, gazed into the fire as though she were reading the future in its fitful embers.

No wonder that the child, used only to tenderness, looked fearfully upon that pale, dark face, grown prematurely old. Her hair still hung over her shoulders, a long and tangled mass, all its purple luster, all its beauty gone forever. There was a strange, wild look about the eyes, and under them a dark, sunken circle. Far into the night she sat brooding over the glowing embers, till they were turned to blackened cinders.

That night Catrina had a more pleasant dream than she had known since her father died.

After the little one had eaten her supper, Catrina undressed her, and wrapping her in a blanket, placed her in her own bed, patting her caressingly with her hand till she fell asleep.

Catrina lay down beside her, and soon she dreamed that an angel came to the cottage and changed the darkness to light, that even her step-mother's face grew gentle and tender, and her voice soft and low in that blessed presence. Her own weary heart grew light, and as she looked fondly at this angel, full of gratitude for her new-born happiness, she saw only the child before her, but clearly she heard these words, in the well-remembered tones of her father's voice, saying:—

"This child shall be the angel of the house." She awoke to find her face bathed in tears, and kissed the baby a hundred times, and in her silence prayed God to bless the darling.

Already the joy of an angel's presence filled her heart. Poor little Catrina! She

was only a child of ten years, yet her face
looked pinched, old, and careworn. This
was not strange for the work of the cottage
fell to her small hands, and there was no
one to say: "You have done well, my little
Catrina."

She could not remember her own gentle
mother, nor when the step-mother came to
them, but she never forgot the sad face of
the dear papa, when he used to pat his
hand upon her tangled hair, saying: "Catrina, you will miss papa; no one else but
my poor little desolate *Mijita mia, Mijita
mia.*" Then he would turn to hide the tears
that would not be driven back. In those
days of illness he was helpless as Catrina
in her babyhood.

One day, when the step-mother had been
gone since the dawning, the father seemed
to sleep, Catrina sat very silently for many
hours, for young as she was, she did not

wish to disturb poor sick papa when sleeping. She grew very weary, but still he did not wake; so she ran softly to the bedside, and looked at him till her heart grew faint. He lay so still, and was very pale; and when she climbed up and laid her little face against his, she shuddered and wept bitterly, it was so very cold. After a while the step-mother returned. Soon some men came and took the father away, and though they looked very rough, one of them stopped and gave her a tortilla, saying: " Poor little young one, she has lost her best friend."

As soon as the little girl could do any thing, the step-mother gave her plenty of work. Thus the years went by till the eve of the *fête* of Corpus Christi, when baby Gracia was brought to the cottage.

It seemed like the dawn of a new life to

the lonely Catrina to look into that sweet
baby face, and when the little one learned
to love her and cry for her, though she
found her task much heavier, her heart
grew so light that her little hands worked
wonders.

The woman took off the pretty coral
necklace and sleeve clasps, and all the
child's fine clothes, and placed them in the
strong oaken chest at the head of her bed.
Little Gracia was dressed in clothes coarse
as Catrina's, but still she grew more lovely
every day, and looked like a little princess
in her rags.

Even the seared heart of the woman softened to the winning ways of the pretty
child, though sometimes she would drive
her away, exclaiming: "Go, go from me—
I hate the race." At other times she would
take her in her arms, saying: "The baby
is not to blame," and with tears dimming

her eyes, cover the little face with fond caresses.

*　　　*　　　*　　　*　　　*　　　*

Thus passed five long years at the cottage. Catrina had grown stronger, and more shapely. Her face was full of love and tenderness, though exposure had made her skin very rough and brown. Gracia had changed from babyhood to a sportive child, graceful as a young fawn.

One rainy night the woman came home very late, leaning heavily upon the arm of an old Indian, who with great difficulty supported her trembling steps. She was very ill, and she felt the cold shadow of death falling upon her.

Gracia was asleep, but Catrina sat by the fire waiting, and keeping the supper hot. She was frightened when she saw the pale face of the step-mother, and trem-

bled with fear as she helped the Indian
to lay her upon the bed.

For a few moments the sick woman was
silent from exhaustion, but after a time
she called Catrina to her.

"Listen to me, Catrina, for my time is
growing short. I have been cruel to you
at times, but you have been always good
and true. Forgive me now, my poor Catrina as you pray the good Lord to forgive
you."

Here the woman grew so faint that
she was obliged to stop speaking, and
Catrina wept as though her heart would
break.

Poor girl! she had been hardly used,
but she knew no other fate; and though
she did not love the step-mother as she did
the little Gracia, it seemed very desolate
to sit there by the dying woman who had
given her a home, poor though it was.

She pressed the cold hand to her lips, and buried her head in the bed-clothes.

"Oh! that child!" gasped the wretched woman. "Catrina, I have no time to lose. I see every thing so differently.

"I have been crazy, but all is clear now. Catrina, when you think of me remember me only as a poor suffering woman, and forgive me, as you hope for God's mercy.

"But the child! in that trunk you will find her clothes and papers which will prove her birth. Her father is a good and true man, as I have learned this day. My life's great wrong came from another's hand.

"Promise me, Catrina, that you will never rest till you have restored her to her home, and the parents who love her."

The step-mother's words grew fainter, but her eyes, full of the brightness of expiring fires, were fixed upon Catrina, who reverently made the sign of the cross, and bowed her head in solemn acquiescence.

"Catrina," she continued, "go up to the cañon, keeping to the right, then over the mountain path, till you come to the great wood." A spasm of pain convulsed her, and she ceased speaking. In a few moments it passed away, and a calm happy smile settled upon her face.

" I repent of all my sins; I forgive even the murderer of him who was dearer than my life. Now, may God have mercy upon my soul."

The husky voice was hushed, the clasped hands relaxed, and the suffering woman was dead!

" She has gone to the land of the Great Spirit, and He has blessed her," said the Indian, filled with amazement to see the troubled face grow so calm in death.

They buried her in the shadow of the deep cañon, and the children were left alone. The kind Indian came every day to the cottage to look after them, bringing always a bag of tortillas and fruits.

One morning, about a week after the death of the step-mother, he found Catrina and Gracia just leaving the cottage. As he gave Catrina the tortillas she shook his hand long and kindly, and the tears glistened in her eyes, but she could not speak to tell him she was going away, never to rest, until she had led Gracia back to her home.

For many days the Indian returned with his bag of tortillas, and went sadly away, for the cottage was alone in the dusky shadows.

The children took the path to the right out of the cañon, then on up the steep mountain way. Catrina carried Gracia's

baby-clothes in her arms, and a large bag
of tortillas, for she had eaten sparingly for
a week, that she might have food for a
long journey.

After awhile Gracia became weary, and
then Catrina took her in her arms, though
they seemed full, but the willing heart
found a ready way to help her darling.

At last they reached the top of the
mountain, so very worn and weary, that
after they had eaten their dinners, Gracia
fell heavily upon Catrina's lap, but she
could no longer support the weight of the
child; so, folding her in her arms, they lay
down upon the soft turf together and slept
as soundly as though it had been a bed of
down.

The shadows were growing very long
when the young girls awoke, and all the
west was glowing with fleecy amber
clouds. The sunset in the clear pure

atmosphere of the mountains seemed so
much more rich and beautiful than in the
dim cañon, that little Gracia's eyes shone
with delight.

"Oh! Catrina," she exclaimed, "surely
that is the glorious heaven we see before
us. Do you not remember what the good
padre told us, when he came to the cottage? Let us hurry, Catrina, 'tis not so
very far. Perhaps we can get there before
dark."

Catrina caught the hand of the excited
child, and making the sign of the cross,
knelt down with her face toward the sunset, and prayed for the soul of the unhappy step-mother, for the little Gracia,
whom she loved dearly, and last of all for
herself.

The radiance of the sunset fell upon the
poor dumb girl, and shed its shining
beauty upon her face. When Catrina

arose, Gracia looked at her with eyes full
of eager wonder.

"How God loves you, Catrina," she
whispered. "He threw his glory all
around you when you prayed." Catrina
smiled and kissed the child, and giving
her a tortilla, they began to descend the
mountain, but the twilight came on so fast
that very soon they could hardly see their
way.

Gracia clasped Catrina's hand very
closely, saying: "I should be afraid in the
dark, only God loves you so much, and
heaven is so near."

Thus they went on as long as they could
see, and then sat down in the darkness,
and by and by slept again.

Catrina woke early in the morning, and
seeing a lime-tree not far distant, covered
with fruit, left Gracia sleeping, and ran to
gather some. "It will be so nice with our

dry tortillas," she thought; "and dear Gracia will be pleased with the juicy fruit."

She made great haste, fearing lest the child might wake, and be frightened at her absence, and in a short time she returned with her apron filled with the delicious fruit. Her face lighted with the smile of grateful love, as she saw the little girl still sleeping sweetly. A moment more and the happy smile was turned to an expression of intense horror.

Only a few feet from the child crouched the huge form of an immense cougar, his fierce eyes gloating with hungry fire upon his helpless prey.

Catrina remained transfixed for a moment, watching the wild beast, until he crouched to spring upon her darling; she then threw her arms over her head, rushed forward, and by what means, God knows, her intense terror burst the prison-

5

bonds of sound, and the dumb girl gave one wild, shrill cry, that made the mountains echo.

Just at that moment came a sharp flash of light, and the cougar lay weltering in his blood.

The startled Gracia woke to find Catrina lying as one dead upon the ground, and a handsome young boy coming forward to help them. The little girl was much frightened, and, weeping bitterly, she threw her arms around Catrina and called piteously,—

"Oh, Catrina! Catrina! open your eyes; do not leave me, Catrina; God loves you, He has called you!"

Then Catrina opened her eyes, and said, with imperfect utterance, "Don't cry, my darling. The cougar is dead. Don't cry; he will not hurt you." And she kissed Gracia, and cried as hard as the child.

"You! Catrina, you speak!" exclaimed little Gracia, as soon as she could speak, for Catrina's caresses.

"You speak, who never spoke in your life. The good God heard your prayer last night. He shed His glory upon you, and now you speak." They embraced each other, and wept for joy.

Then they noticed the handsome boy standing near them, resting upon his gun, and Catrina pressed his hand to her lips, and thanked him again and again.

They all went to look at the cougar together, and Catrina told the wondering Gracia how very near to heaven she had been, and young Leon De Laude told them both how he had started by moonlight to hunt in the mountains, and how he thanked God he had been able to save the little señorita.

They sat down to eat their tortillas

and fruit, and then started for the valley.
Poor Catrina! How delightful to be
able to talk, though she needed practice
to be able to speak plainly.

She was like a little child just learning,
but she managed to let Leon know all
about Gracia, and he, with delighted
surprise, told her that he knew her father,
who was the richest señor in all the country, and that in a few hours they could
reach the vineyard.

Never were there happier young people
than went down the mountain together.
As they entered the wood, whom should
they meet but poor old nurse, Macata,
hunting for her lost darling.

"I have found the little señorita for you,
good Macata," said Leon. Macata gave
one glance at Gracia, then caught her in
her arms, exclaiming, "*Ninita mia! Ninita
mia! Waconda!* the Master of Life has

heard my cry! I knew you were not lost
for ever."

The old Indian started off at full speed,
carrying Gracia in her arms, sobbing all
the time, and blessing the Great Spirit
that she had lived to restore the lost child
to the dear señora.

Leon and Catrina could barely keep pace
with her, but at last they entered the very
room, where, five years before, the beautiful
child lay sleeping in her little willow
cradle.

" I have brought her back, señora," cried
old Macata, out of breath. " It is our little
white bud, señora, dear! Oh! *Alma mia!
Mijita mia*, Waconda has not forgotten
us!" The old woman placed the child in
the mother's arms, and fell with her face
upon the floor, weeping for joy.

No words can tell the joy that filled the
house. Only the heart of the father and

mother could feel how greatly God had blessed them.

Now the years went pleasantly by. The good Catrina become a lovely maiden. Her form gained strength and beauty. Her hair grew soft and glossy; her skin clear and smooth, and her brown eyes were tender with the light of happiness. But, most wonderful of all, her voice was a marvel of sweetness. It was a great pleasure to hear her sing at evening, accompanied by the soft music of her light guitar. She was loved by all, but especially so by the young hidalgo, who won her for his bride.

Leon and Gracia danced together at the wedding, and it was plain enough to see how devoted the brave young señor was to the graceful señorita whose life he had saved.

Gracia had grown more and more beautiful every year, till in all the country she was called *La Bonita*.

She had many admirers, but the señor said, " Young Leon restored her to us, and to him only will we give our child." Thus, upon her sixteenth birthday, the great wedding feast was made, and all San Diego around re-echoed the great joy. There were tables spread under the lime-trees for the poor, and all the country was there.

In the quaint adobe church the marriage ceremony was performed, and with a happy heart Leon received his bride, while the father and mother thanked God for His most blessed gifts, their son and daughter. Thus all their sorrows ended, and all their lives were circled by the light of happiness and love.

THE DANCING SUNBEAM.

IN a dark, narrow street of the city stood
a dingy tenement house. Many people lived
within, and called it by the dear name of
home; yet it was very different from the
luxurious homes of the rich, surrounded
by pleasant gardens, filled with costly pictures, and a thousand beautiful things very
delightful to possess. Nor was it like the
comfortable homes of the middle class,
where the fire burns brightly in the polished grate, and the table is always plenti-
fully spread. Oh, no! The people in the
tenement house were all poor, from the
first floor front to the attic back, which
was the worst of all.

It was the rainy season, and through

the roof, round the chimney, and between
the cracked and loosened weather-boards,
came the driving rain.

Then there was a continual opening and
shutting of doors; and at the common en-
trance, all day long and far into the night,
there was somebody always coming in, or
going out, letting in the chilling blast, that
rushed through the muddy halls, and into
the rooms, pinching the sick and old in a
pitiless way.

Altogether, it was not a pleasant place
to live in; but most of the people in the
tenement house had always been poor, and
had learned to be content with what the
day brought them, so they were not hungry. Only one in the house had known
the luxury of being very rich, and she was
now the poorest of them all.

Just under the roof she sat, wearily
stitching upon the coarse work that must

bring bread to her little child.   How the
rain pattered and clattered upon the roof,
as the daintily-bred woman bent above her
unaccustomed task, thinking over the old
thoughts, that made the present more than
desolate.

"It was not so once," said the rain.
"The old home, how comfortable and
beautiful it was! There you were a fair
lady with lily-white hands; now, you are
the same, only one can not think so.
There are silver threads in your hair, and
your hands are too red. People say:
'What a pity the woman with the pretty
child is so poor!' but they do not help
you."

"The old home! the old home!" echoed
the sad thoughts all day long and into the
still hours of the night.

In the corner of the room sat a little
child, playing with a doll, made of an old

apron; yet, to the child it was "the pretty Dolladine."

She was very beautiful, with silken white hair, shimmered over with a golden luster. A little garden flower, thrown out by chance upon the common wayside, yet blossoming in her own sweet beauty, in contrast with every thing around her.

She was a real princess born, and her coarse, ragged clothes could make no difference.

The work was finished, and, though it was raining still, the mother put on her worn bonnet to take it home.

"If the sun would only shine again," she sighed heavily, looking down into the dismal back alley; "but I must go."

She kissed the child, saying, "Be good, darling—mamma will not be gone long."

"I will be good, mamma," she answered,

"and Dolladine and I will catch the sunshine for you."

"You are my only sunshine now," said the mother, hastening away to conceal the tears that would not stay in their hiding-place.

Then the little one was left alone in the attic-room, and began, as she often did, to talk to her doll.

"Now, Dolladine," she said, "mamma is very sad, and sick, I fear, and you and I must make sunshine for her; but how shall we do it? that is the question.

"Don't you remember, Dolladine, one day the pretty lady said my hair was beaming sunshine? We must shake it out for poor mamma—we must shake it out;" and the little girl began jumping around the room, shaking her curls, and singing :—

> "We will make the bright sunshine,
>   Dolladine, Dolladine ;
> Make for mamma glad sunshine,
>   Dolladine, Dolladine."

Just then she saw the sunbeams dancing into the room. The rain was over, and, on the roof of the next house, a washer-woman was hanging out her clothes, which were blowing about in the wind, casting gleams of light and shadow upon the little attic window, so that the sunshine went flitting about like the will-o'-the-wisp, for the shadow was always chasing it.

The child was delighted. "Do you see it, Dolladine," she said—"the glorious sunshine which the loving God gives us? Now, we must catch it for mamma."

She took the doll in her arms, and gave chase to the dancing phantom. But it was no use; just as her little hand was ready to grasp it, it flew away.

"You don't help me enough, Dolladine," said the child, her little eyes filling with tears.

Just then, a great double-knock came at

the door, and, before she could answer it, in walked a little old man, with a very wrinkled face and long white beard; a big hat almost covered his face, so that the upper part was all in shadow.

"What are you doing, little chick?" he said, pleasantly; "and where is the mother?"

"Mamma has gone to carry home the work," answered the child, timidly; "and Dolladine and I have been making sunshine for her. But, see! it flies away!" and again she tried to catch the dancing beams.

"It often does from older and wiser hands than yours; but how did you make it, fairy?" asked the old man, laughing.

"God put it in my hair, and I shook it out for dear mamma, who is sick, and so tired of the dark days," replied the little one, again shaking her pretty curls, that were luminous with beauty.

" I see!" said the old man. "Now, I am
a great magician, and can help you;" and
he sang, with a clear, ringing voice :—

> " Sunshine, sunshine, flitting and airy,
>   Dwell in the heart of the little fairy;
>   Make her gentle. loving. and mild,
>   Make her the mother's sunshine child."

Just at that moment the washerwoman
took down a big sheet, and the little room
was flooded with warm, glowing sunshine.

" Oh! it is glorious, is it not, Dolladine?" exclaimed the child, clapping her
hands, and dancing about with pleasure.
" Mamma will be so happy, and so will
Dolladine and I."

" Remember," said the old magician,
" that all good comes from the loving God,
who has blessed you, and made you the
sunshine child. You can make the mother
and every one very happy, so long as you

keep God's sunshine in your heart; but if
you forget the blessed Christ, it will fly
away, and will not be the warm, beautiful
light of God's love, but only the dancing
sunshine that always escapes your grasp.
And then, how sad! you would change
to the little stormy-weather child, which
would be worse than the darkest winter's
day to the dear mother."

"Oh! no, no! I will never forget to
bless the good God. It is so delightful to
make mamma and every one happy."

"This box," said the old man, "is full
of sunshine; I will give it you for the
mother."

"Let me kiss you, dear magician," said
the child, gently; "I always love anybody
who is kind to poor mamma."

The old man took the little one in
his arms, and kissed her fondly, saying,
"God bless you, darling; God bless you!"

Then he went away, to be her life-long
friend.

"I am so happy, I can not keep still,
Dolladine," said the child; and she danced
about till the mother came in, weary and
worn. "Oh! mamma," said she, running
up and kissing her, "we shall always be
happy now, in God's glorious sunshine,
and the old magician gave me this box,
full of it, for you, mamma."

It was some time before the mother
could understand all; but when she opened the box, sure enough, it was full of
sunshine. There was the missing deed,
that restored to her her own—the dear old
home, and all her great wealth.

Again she became the fair lady with the
lily-white hands; but her greatest joy was
in the warm, genial sunshine her good
little daughter made. From a child she
grew up to be a loving, beautiful, and

pure woman. But she never forgot the good God, and, all her life, remained the mother's sunshine child.

•

THE YOUNG GOLD-SEEKER.

In the olden time, between the Mission of San Gabriel and Los Angeles, lived an old Spaniard, his wife, and one son.

In his early manhood, Don Pedro had been very rich, but sickness and misfortune had followed him, until, in his old age, he was destitute of many of the comforts of life.

Sorrowful and dispirited, he looked forward to death as the only portal of hope for future repose.

Francisco, his son, was full of youthful ambition and ardent life.

One morning he went to the bedside of his father and mother, and kneeling down beside them begged their blessing.

"I am going," he said, "dear father and mother, to retrieve your fallen fortunes."

The father blessed him, and bade him Godspeed, but the mother wept and clasped her arms about him, till her silver hair mingled with the glossy black of his; and when he tore himself regretfully from her embrace, she called him again and again to return for one more kiss. At last, when he rushed out, and was nearly gone from her, she buried her head in the bed-clothes and sobbed as if her heart would break.

Francisco was at first greatly saddened and subdued by his dear mother's grief; but soon with the fresh morning air, the elastic spirits of youth, rose joyous and hopeful, and he sung merrily as he wandered on through the open country.

He had taken with him some tortillas (coarse Indian-meal cakes) and dried beef.

When he was hungry, he sat down in the shade, ate sparingly of these and of the delicious fruits that abound through all the country, and drank from the clear spring.

Thus passed the first few days of his journeying; but there came a time, when, out in the desert, his food became exhausted, and there were no cooling springs bubbling up from the yellow heat of the burning sand.

There were no trees, no fruit, no shade. He wandered on for two days and nights, until nature was almost exhausted, and when the third night came, he threw himself upon the sand to die.

He prayed devoutly to the Holy Virgin to intercede for his soul, and grant his fevered body rest; when, as he turned his head wearily, far out on the desert gleamed a light.

Hope rose in his bosom, and he drew his

aching limbs onward, till nearer and nearer gleamed the blessed light from a cool oasis in the desert. Soon his foot pressed the soft turf, and green trees waved above his head.

The blessed Virgin had pitied him and listened to his prayer. He was saved.

He thought the waters of the running stream the sweetest music he had ever heard, and bending over, with his hand he raised to his parched lips a draught of holy water—for 'twas the Mother of Mercy's gift—the gift of life.

Extreme thirst is the most intolerable of all sufferings—greater far than hunger. None but those who have endured its pangs, can have the least idea of the excruciating pain it brings.

After Francisco had drank the water, he was for a time very sick, but soon was sufficiently relieved to long for food and

rest, so again he looked for the light that
had guided him to the oasis.

Just before him, from the thicket of palm-
trees it gleamed. He drew near cautiously,
fearing it might prove the encampment of
hostile Indians.

Softly as he stepped, the quick ear of an
old Indian woman detected his approach,
and she raised her eyes to meet his eager
and hungry gaze, as he looked longingly at
the supper she was preparing over the fire
just outside her little cane hut.

When he saw that he was discovered, he
went up to her, holding out his hand, and
saying :—

"Good mother, I am very hungry and
weary, give me something to eat and let me
rest here to-night, or I shall die. Oh,
mother! mother!"

He was thinking of his own mother at
home; but his words and tones sunk into

the heart of the old Indian woman, and
tears gathered in her dim eyes as she
placed her hand softly on Francisco's
shoulders.

"You call me mother," she said, in
Spanish, sadly, "those who used to call me
mother are all dead! My boy would have
been like you. My brave boy! my timid
girl, gone! all gone!"

She wept bitterly as she gave Francisco
the choicest morsels, and a cool, delicious
drink, that was a balm to his parched and
aching throat.

When Francisco had eaten, he was overcome with fatigue and want of sleep, but
when he would have thrown himself down
upon a mat in the hut, and fallen asleep
immediately, the old mother caught him by
the arm, exclaiming:—

"You must not lie down there to sleep,
you would never wake again; for when the

chief, my husband, returns, he would kill you, for he hates the Spaniards. What can I do with you, my poor boy ?"

"I can go no farther, mother, I shall die of fatigue if I try ; think of the two days and nights I passed upon the desert, without food, drink or sleep." And he threw himself in the corner, saying : " he must kill me if he will," and in a moment was fast asleep.

The old woman bent over and kissed him, weeping.

" He called me mother," she said, "poor boy, poor boy."

She covered him over with cool boughs, with the thick green leaves still fresh upon them.

How long he slept he could not tell, but while it was yet dark, a rough voice very near, awoke him.

Opening his eyes and peering through

the mass of foliage, he saw a gigantic Indian, surrounded by half a dozen younger men, all eating what appeared to be an early breakfast, and talking over some adventure in which they were about engaging.

From their conversation he learned that he was approaching the borders of the rich Arizona country; and he noticed, when the chief put up his ammunition (he was the only one who carried a gun), that the bullet was of pure gold.

He lay for some time motionless, carefully watching their movements. At one time he came very near being discovered.

One of the young Indians had mislaid his bow and arrow, and went to the pile of brush to look for it; but the old woman, whose mother's heart had warmed to the perishing young stranger, drove the Indian boy away, with a sharp reproof for his carelessness in disturbing her basket of reeds, which were mingled with the concealing boughs.

At last the missing bow was found, and the company mounted and rode away.

Again silence fell upon the palm-shaded hut.

Still weary, Francisco lay quietly watching the old woman, as she moved about with a lighted taper, silently putting the things to rights; but at last she blew out the light, and lay down to rest upon a mat near the door, and in the darkness, the green oasis of the desert faded into the land of dreams.

The morning sun was shining clear and bright, through the waving branches of the palm-trees, when Francisco again awoke.

There was no one in the hut when he arose and went to the spring, where the night before he had slaked his thirst.

Again he drank from its pure fountain,

bathing his face and neck in the sparkling water, till he felt quite refreshed.

Above his head, amid the glossy leaves hung the rich yellow bananas.

He gathered some and ate them as he returned to the hut, with a hopeful, happy heart.

The old mother met him at the door, and greeted him pleasantly.

They sat down together and ate their morning meal. Francisco told her how he had left home to seek his fortune, and of his father and mother, who had once been very rich, and had become poor, and in their old age were suffering for the comforts of life. How he had vowed, if his life was spared, that they should enjoy all that money and love could provide for them. "And now, mother," he said, " I am seeking gold, and gold I must have, if my life pays the forfeit."

"Were it not that the chieftain, my husband, would kill you, I could show you where gold is plenty enough," said the old woman. "Only one day's journey from here are the great mines, and even on the ground you can pick up quite large nuggets of almost pure gold; but every hour you stay here your life is in danger, and you must live to be happy.

"There are places in the Arizona country where the ground is yellow with gold. The Indians care little for it, but you could never go there and return alive. At every step your way would be beset with a more deadly foe than the hunger and thirst of the desert.

"Boy, you have wakened a love that was dead in my heart. I will save you if possible, and, as nearly as I can will grant your wishes."

Then the old woman prepared food and

water for a journey, and taking two deer-skin bags, she filled them with great nuggets of pure gold, and laid across the back of a strong mule, as much as he could carry, and embracing Francisco, she bade him take the mule and recross the desert with all possible dispatch.

"To-night our men will return, and you must be far away."

Then she gave him directions about the way. "By to-night, if you keep the trail, you will reach green trees and water. Go home now, be rich and happy; but some times remember the lonely Indian mother far away in Arizona."

The old woman embraced him again, weeping, and said: "All who call me mother must go from me."

Francisco kissed her brown cheek, and went out from under the shade of the palm trees into the arid waste.

Looking back, as long as he could see over the desert, in the distance he saw the old woman watching him. She, too, had gone out from the shadow of the palm-trees, and stood upon the burning sand, shading her tearful eyes with her wrinkled hand from the blinding sunshine.

God pity the childless mother.

Francisco was fortunate in keeping the trail, and at night reached the trees and water the old woman had spoken of, but the desert was still before him—a long and toilsome journey.

For six weary days he traveled through an arid sandy waste, finding water at intervals; and when at last the green hills of San Gabriel rose before him, he wept like a child for joy; but he soon called back his manhood and laughed at his weakness.

With a full happy heart he journeyed on, till Los Angeles, dear Los Angeles, the home of his infancy, lay before him. There was the cottage of his mother, and she herself standing at the door. He had returned after all his hardships, strong, rich, and happy. Again the gray hair of his mother rested on his shoulder, but this time she wept tears of joy, as he whispered in her ear: "Mother, dear! you and father can never want again, I am rich now. I have gold enough to last a lifetime; and, mother, you shall have a beautiful home: and I will ask Juanita, who loves you, to come and be your daughter and my wife."

THE WISHING-CAP.

THROUGH the branches of a great almond-tree sported the golden sunlight, till it fell in shining flecks upon the broad verandas of a spacious adobe house. Nothing could be pleasanter than this homestead in the southern Gold Land, with the great garden around it, filled with all kinds of tropical flowers and fruits in their season. Here dwelt a little boy and girl, whose father and mother were both dead, so they, poor children, had their sorrows.

After the mother died, the father had married a poor widow, who had two children, about the age of his own little ones.

At first, while the comfort of the new home was a novelty to the woman, she

6*

had been kind to the children; but, as the strangeness wore off, she began to feel like the real mistress. In a thousand ways she favored her own children, who were proud and selfish; and in all their childish differences, only the motherless ones were punished.

Then the father died, and the step-mother became like a great shadow between them and the bright sunshine of childhood. She would have sent them away from home, but their own mother had been very rich, and, after the father's death, the house in which they lived, the vineyard, and the large herd of cattle feeding upon the hills, all belonged to them.

The step-mother was very angry at this, but she was their guardian, so she managed every thing to suit herself, and lived in great ease and luxury.

One day, as the children were playing

in the garden, the step-mother's son threw his ball into a wild-rosebush that was covered with thorns.

"Go and get it for me, Zoie," said he, sharply, to the little girl.

"I can not," replied the child, "for the thorns will tear my dress, and the señora will whip me."

"How dare you call my mother the señora? It is not from respect, but because you are a hateful little beast." And he struck the child a cruel blow, and made her go for the ball.

Her dress was torn, and her pretty hands bleeding when she recovered it. Just then her own brother came up, and would have fought the unkind boy, but the little Zoie entreated, weeping, "Dear brother, do not strike him. Come with me, while I say, 'Forgive us our trespasses, as we forgive those who trespass against us.'"

The heart of the young boy swelled
with anger, and his quickened pulse beat
fearfully; but, because he loved his sister,
he suffered her to lead him away, for well
he knew, nothing would grieve her so
much as his returning blow for blow.

"Oh! to be a man!" he thought, as the
hot tears filled his eyes. "Why don't the
years fly fast? How long must I wait, before I can take care of my little sister like
a man?"

Already the manhood was dawning in
his heart; and if he could have protected
the dear little maiden, he would have
dared any thing.

At this moment the garden gate opened,
and an old Indian woman came up the
walk, crying—"Strawberries! fresh and
ripe, red and bright. Strawberries! strawberries!"

All the children ran to meet her, and

looked so eagerly at the pretty crimson fruit, that she gave to each of them a handful, but to the little sister, who was so modest and beautiful, she gave a small basket, covered with green leaves, and filled with the delicious berries.

When the other children would have taken the basket for themselves, the old woman prevented them; and, while they went, crying, to their mother, Zoie hid her treasure under the trailing vines of a passion-flower.

" Be quick, little señorita," said the old Indian. " Your mother once saved the life of my child, and an Indian never forgets. In the basket is a wonderful talisman, which will give you any thing you want, just for the wishing."

She had hardly time to say this, when the step-mother came out, and bought all the fruit she had left.

The señora was very angry with the orphans, and, after whipping them both for quarreling, sent them supperless to bed, in an old out-house where the Indian servants slept, but she and her children sat down to a luxurious meal, with a large basket of delicious strawberries in the center of the table, plenty of nice white sugar, and three bowls of fresh, rich cream.

For some time the lonely orphans lay talking of their own dear parents, and weeping, as they lay shivering in each other's arms. The evening was coming on, and, though the days were very warm, there was a chill in the damp night air, and they had only a thin sheet to cover them.

At last the brother said: "Sister, I can not endure it. If they would only whip me—but to see them strike you! I can not endure it! You, whom I promised the

dear papa to love and protect. We have
nothing but sorrow here. Let us go out
into the wide world alone. It will not be
so bad—at least we shall be away from
the señora, who gives only hard crusts
to eat."

"Dear brother, let us go! The good
God, who takes care of the pretty birds,
will take care of us. But first bring me
my blue shawl, for it was the last thing
the dear mamma gave me."

Very softly the boy rose and went for
the shawl, but the old Indian cook, who
had lived in the family before he was
born, and loved the children dearly, saw
him, and gave him some tortillas.

"The old wizzen witch, to treat the real
señora's children so!" said the woman, angrily. "She, the señora, to be sure! A
cane hut in the chaparral would be good
enough for her."

"Good-bye, mammie," said the boy, throwing his arms around the old Indian's neck; " we are going away to seek our fortune, and when I am a man, you shall live with us. But do not follow us now, or she will see you. We are running away from the señora," he whispered softly.

The old Indian pressed him to her heart for a moment, and then said, " Go! for nothing in the wild woods will hurt you so much as staying here. I shall go to-morrow, but I must wait and see that the old witch does not bring you back, for I believe she would kill you, only for me."

Then the boy went softly out, and the old Indian covered her face with her apron, and thought over her half savage thoughts, which were still full of good faith and love to the children who had slept in her bosom in their helpless infancy.

The little Zoie was waiting for her

brother in the garden. As soon as she saw him, she held up the basket of strawberries, saying, "This is all we have, but, no doubt in the wide world, God will give us all we need."

The young boy wrapped the shawl about her, and, clasping each other's hands, they stole out of the garden silently, but, when the gate had closed upon them, he told her how the old cook had given them the tortillas.

"That is but the beginning of our good fortune," answered the child.

As they passed the Lake of the Tuleis, the moon and stars were shining pleasantly, casting a flood of soft golden light upon the graves of the father and mother. Here the children stopped for a moment, and the little maiden laid her head upon the green grave of the mother, crying— "Oh, mamma, mamma! We loved you so dearly, and are so lonely now. We are going out into the wide world alone, mamma! dear, sweet mamma!"

She buried her head in the long grass, and there would have wept herself to sleep, as she had often done before, but the brother took her by the hand, saying, "We must hasten, sister, or the señora will come after us."

So they ran on as fast as they could, and every waving shrub or tree their fear and the darkness changed into the form of the angry step-mother.

At last they came to a thick wood, and began to feel quite safe as they entered it. It seemed so large, and so far out into the wide world, that they were sure the step-mother could never find them there.

The gray twilight of the morning was coming on, and, as they were very tired and hungry, they sat down under the trees

to eat their tortillas and strawberries. In
the bottom of the basket Zoie found a nut,
about the size of an almond. " This must
be the talisman that makes wishing ' having,' " said the little girl.

They wished all sorts of things, but
nothing came to them, and the boy said,
" It is a poor talisman—throw it away."

" No, brother," answered the child; " the
old woman was so kind to me, for her sake
I will keep it always, and who knows
what may come of it yet?"

So she wrapped it in a leaf, and placed
it in her bosom. Then they said their
prayers, and, covering themselves with the
shawl, they slept soundly till morning.

When they awoke, the sun was shining
through the leaves of a rich banana tree,
and the ripe golden fruit was hanging in
thick bunches just above their heads.

" See, brother," said the little girl, " the

good God has given us our breakfast;"
and they gathered from the ground as
much of the delicious fruit as they
wished.

" I am so thirsty," said the brother.

" I hear something that sounds like running water," replied Zoie.

So they looked around, until they found
a brook, with a clear spring of water bubbling up in the midst of the shining
stones.

" I thank the good God for this pure,
clear water," said the little girl, drinking
with much pleasure, for she, too, was beginning to be very thirsty.

" We must go now," said the boy.

They each took as many bananas as
they could carry, and started to go, they
knew not whither.

They were light-hearted and happy in
all their morning wanderings, but by noon

they began to feel tired, hungry, and thirsty.

"I am sorry we left the beautiful shady banana tree and the brook. It is so hot, and I am very thirsty," said the boy, sadly. So they both looked for water, but could find none.

"God will give us some by and by," said the little sister. "Let us sit down and eat our dinner."

They ate their bananas with sad hearts, and the wide world seemed very desolate. All around them the grass was withered, and the trees and shrubs were dying for want of water.

Though they were so much fatigued, and it was very warm, they were too thirsty to think of rest, and all the afternoon they wandered about looking for water and finding none.

By and by the twilight came on, then

the stars and the great golden moon shone upon the pale face of the children, glistening with tears.

"What shall we do, sister," said the boy, weeping, and falling upon the ground in despair; "we shall die, we can not be buried by the Lake of the Tuleis, with the dear papa and mamma."

"Do not cry, brother," said the little Zoie, her own eyes filling with tears. "I am sure God will help us, and if he lets us die here, he will send the birds to cover us with leaves, as they did the poor little 'children in the woods.'"

She put her arms around her brother's neck, and kissed him, saying again, "Do not cry, dear, God *will* help us, he is our 'Father who art in heaven.'"

So they started again, and very soon they saw a tiny light shining through the trees, and as they ran forward it grew

brighter, and clearer, and they heard a
very pleasant sound, the rushing of waters.

Taking heart again, they urged their
little weary feet forward, till they came to
a mill, and the clear light shone from the
comfortable room, in which sat the weary
miller, by a glowing fire, while his young
son prepared the supper.

They knocked timidly at the door, and
a rough kind voice said, " Come in."

They entered, and saw the miller sitting
by the fire, and his handsome young son
spreading the table.

The old man spoke to them, but they
could not understand him, for he spoke in
English, and they were Spanish children;
but the boy said, in the soft Spanish tongue,
" My friends, who are you? and where did
you come from?"

The little girl answered, " We are poor
children, whose papa and mamma are dead,

and God takes care of us. We are very
hungry and thirsty, and he showed us the
light shining from your window, so we are
here!"

Then the boy gave them milk to drink,
and put two more plates on the table, while
he told the father what the children said.

"Bless her innocent heart," said the old
man, "God's little ones are welcome."

He took the child in his arms, and she
nestled her head down in his rough neck,
and whispered, "I love you, you seem like
the dear papa."

A tear came into the old man's eye, he
only understood the word papa, but there
was affection in the little arms that twined
around his neck, and he kissed her, and
said again, "Bless her little heart."

Her winning ways touched his affec-
tionate nature, they made him think of a
lonely grave, and his own lost darling.

Meanwhile the boys talked pleasantly till supper was ready, then they sat down together to a bountiful table, and the hungry children ate heartily, and drank the pure sweet milk, which after their long thirst seemed delicious.

After supper they went to sleep on a nice deer-skin, spread upon the floor, but some how that night the old man could not sleep.

He got up two or three times to look at the children, with the tears standing in his eyes.

He was living over the past. "Bless her little heart," he said, smoothing with his rough hand the soft wavy hair of the little girl.

In the morning the children woke much refreshed. At first they did not know where they were, but they saw the face of the old man turned kindly toward them, and remembered all.

7

At breakfast the brother told their story to the boy, and he interpreted it to the father.

"They shall stay with us," said the old man, with great satisfaction, for he had dreaded parting with the child that had so won his love.

After breakfast they went into the mill, and the handsome boy told the orphans his story, in return.

"Some years ago," he said, "my father and mother came to this country, bringing my little sister and myself.

"Mother and sister died very soon after we arrived, and father and I have lived here alone for many years.

"You can't tell how lonely it was at first," he continued, "and how I used to cry myself to sleep, and poor father was very sad. I am so glad you are going to stay with us."

"God sent us," said the little girl, smiling. And the children were very contented and happy together.

Thus they lived for many years at the old mill.

The little Zoie grew to be a beautiful maiden, as good as fair.

To the old father she was a great blessing, making his home always neat and pleasant.

The two boys were handsome, strong young men, full of energy and life. Every day they roamed over the mountains, prospecting for gold. The old mill was falling to decay, and promised but little in the future.

One evening, when they had returned after a hard day's work, weary and out of heart, they sat down on the stone steps of the old mill to rest themselves. The waters were flowing on with their usual pleasant music, and they were thinking and hoping for the future. When the household work was done Zoie came out and sat by them. To amuse them she told over the old story of the strawberries and the talisman that should make "wishing having."

"Let me see the nut," said the miller's son, and Zoie gave it to him.

Placing it upon the stone door-step, he pressed his heel upon it, and the shell burst open, showing a silken cap of bright crimson, trimmed with cord, and tassal of gold.

They were all greatly surprised, and the miller's son placed it upon Zoie's shining hair.

"How pretty it is," said she. "I wish I had a rose-bush filled with roses of the same color."

She had hardly spoken, before a rose-

bush, covered with beautiful crimson flowers, sprang up at their feet.

Then they knew that the pretty silken
toy was a wonderful wishing-cap, and that
any thing they might desire, could be had
for the wishing.

In the morning, when the young men
went out, Zoie put on the cap, and wished
they might find a mine of great richness.

"Though we could now live without the
trouble of working," she said to the father,
" a rich mine would help hundreds of poor
people, who would find employment in it.
So it would be a real blessing."

While they sat talking, the brother
rushed in, bringing a great nugget of gold,
telling how at last, they had found a mine
of fabulous richness.

Thus, they had every thing they desired,
till one day, the miller's son put on the
cap, and told Zoie, that above every thing

in the world, he wished that she might love him, and consent to be his wife.

The young maiden blushed, and begged for the cap. "It was not quite fair," she said, "in wishing that!" So they talked, as young people will, but it ended in her placing her hand in his, and promising to be his bride.

"And this," as the father said, "was the best wish of all."

The brother was greatly pleased, and said, "Zoie shall be married in the old home." So they all went together to the pleasant adobe house from which they had fled so long ago.

The step-mother was greatly surprised so see them. She had so often reported them dead, that she really began to believe it herself.

She was obliged to give up everything to the true heirs. Thus she and her children became very poor again. Though the brothers and sisters gave her a comfortable house, and provided for her, she was very ungrateful.

She was a disappointed woman, unhappy herself, and making others so around her.

It was a glorious day when the young people were married, and Zoie in her snow-white robes and rich lace vail, was as fair a bride as the sun could shine upon.

All the old friends of the family were invited to the wedding feast, and the old servants taken home again.

Every one was rejoiced to see the orphans enjoying their own—but of them all—no one was so happy as the old miller, and when he kissed the bride after the ceremony, he whispered, " bless your little heart, I could not live without my child." The young bride looked into his face, with beaming eyes, and answered only " my father."

Thus they were all happy, and, through the changing scenes of life, the goodness and faith of the wife and mother, never failed. Like the little maid, Zoie, in the dark night, she trusted, and God always took care of them.

In the early days, many strange things happened. It was the mystical age of romance in the Gold Land, and people seemed to live years in months, or even weeks. Thus a great deal has been forgotten.

In the old countries it was not so, and it may be that some are living even now at "dear Bingen on the Rhine," who remember tenderly the handsome young couple who left their home to seek the alluring treasures of the Gold Land in "the early days."

They were honest peasants in the Father land, but over the waters had floated the marvelous story, how, in the glorious El

7*

Dorado, any one might become a lord of the
soil or a rich miner prince.

This it was that fired the heart of the
father; and as the mother looked upon
their boy, she too was ready to go out into
the great world, though her heart lay fondly to the beloved Fatherland.

They had little money, but the thrifty
good-man managed to work for one and
another on the passage, till, when he arrived
at the young city of tents within the Gold-
en Gate, he had cash enough to make a beginning in life.

They were soon domesticated in a little
shanty, and in a short time had prepared a
fine garden, which became the good-man's
pride. Every morning dame Waltenburger
went to the market, where she had a stall,
and sold fruit and vegetables for gold dust,
for that was the currency of the country in
" the early days."

The little son was ten years old, and a real delight to the mother's heart.

He was well formed, with fine features, golden brown hair, and wonderfully expressive eyes. When he was calm and happy they were of a soft looming blue, but if excited or angry, they grew dark and fierce, flashing like balls of fire

It pleased him above all things, to assist the dear mother at the market, and very soon he displayed great taste in the arrangements of the fruits and vegetables.

With maternal pride, the mother often told the neighbors "it would be impossible to do without Paul," for really he was the greatest help to her.

When the flowers were in blossom, the boy always made them into bouquets and garlands, while his pretty ways brought many a purchaser.

Sometimes he used to carry home parcels

for ladies who had made large purchases, and very often he received presents from them. With the regular customers the handsome little fellow was a great favorite.

One day, as Paul and the mother sat in the stall together, talking of the dear Fatherland so far away, they saw a very queer-looking Spanish woman approaching. She seemed bowed down with age and infirmities, and leaned heavily upon her staff as she hobbled along with the greatest difficulty.

After the Spanish fashion her head was covered with a shawl, from which peered her thin sharp face, quite furrowed with wrinkles. Her bleared eyes were red, and her long hooked nose nearly met her pointed chin. Altogether she was very unpleasant in her appearance.

All the time she kept her toothless mouth moving as she mumbled indistinctly to herself.

She came directly up to dame Waltenburger's stall, and entering it, threw herself down upon the bench, exclaiming:
"This is what comes of growing old, nothing
but weariness, care, and aching of bones,'
and she began rubbing her knees and
muttering to herself.

Little Paul stood looking at her, his eyes
dilated with wonder, and the compassion
of his heart made them blue as the cloud-
less sky.

"Ah!" exclaimed the old woman, looking into his innocent face with a hideous
grimace, "what are you staring at, with
your great round owl-eyes? Do you think it
is a fine thing to be old, and lame, and poor?
You will have to come to it. Ah! yes, there
is a comfort in that.

" Old Father Time will take care of you.
Yes! yes! yes!" And she shook her long
bony fingers, and chuckled in such a horrible

way, that the child retreated behind the mother's chair, and hid his face upon her protecting shoulder.

"Go quickly, boy, and bring me some fresh water," said the old woman, "I am very thirsty," she added, looking at the mother.

Little Paul took a glass and ran away to the well and drew a bucket of water, so clear and sparkling that it glistened in the sunlight like the dew of the morning.

As he carried it along, he thought how the professor had told him of shining nectar that Hebe used to bear in the golden cup to Jupiter and all the gods of Olympus.

"That was in the olden time," he said, "but no nectar could be more beautiful and pure than the water the loving God in heaven gives to us all."

Offering it to the old woman, his open rosy face beaming with smiles, he said "it

is nectar fit for the gods, and I am your cup-
bearer."

Then he bowed so prettily that the
mother laughed, saying, "did one ever see
such a child? oh! you mischief, and she
shook her fingers in the cunning old way
that all mothers do."

The old woman took the glass, but
managed to spill half its contents over the
child's clean clothes, then she chuckled with
delight at his discomfiture, saying "see
what it is to be old, my little cup-bearer."

While the mother wiped off the water
with her handkerchief the woman began
picking over the vegetables and fruit with
her thin hooked fingers, and smelling every
bouquet of flowers, till little Paul's eyes
grew dark and flashed like living flames.

"Just see her, mother," he whispered,
"who will buy them after she has handled
every thing with her dirty hands, and snuffed

all the sweetness and beauty out of the flowers with her ugly, crooked nose?"

"Oh, you little viper," cried the old woman, springing forward, "I'll teach you to mock at old age."

Paul was too quick for her, and had it not been for the mother she would have fallen, in her eagerness to catch him.

"Never mind the child, my good woman," said dame Waltenburger, gently, "we were all children once, now how can I serve you?"

"To be sure! we were all children once. Ah! me!

"Oh, no! I don't mind the child, my little cup-bearer," and the old woman drew her wizen face into a hundred wrinkles, and began selecting a large quantity of fruits, vegetables and herbs, far more than she could carry.

"Is it far you have to go?" said the mother.

Crimson Tuft.

"No, no! not far," replied the woman.

So the mother called Paul to help her. He was very reluctant to go; but, when the mother kissed him, and promised to make him a beautiful ball, and cover it with red morocco, he came forward and took the basket readily.

"And I," said the old woman, "will give him a beautiful crimson tuft; he will be gay as a lark, my little cup-bearer."

This seemed delightful to Paul, and he followed after the old woman, thinking— "I can play soldier with the crimson tuft, and the professor in the next house will hear me, and call me Charlemagne. It will be glorious to be the soldier with the crimson tuft."

Little Paul walked on in quite a lordly way, with his great martial thoughts echoing in all the chambers of his boyish heart,

"It will be glorious—the soldier of the crimson tuft!"

On, on they went, far out into the sand hills, in an opposite direction from his own home.

Paul's arm began to ache very much, carrying the heavy basket, but he was feeling so manly, that he did not like to complain; but at last he became so tired, that it was no use—he could not bear it any longer, and great tears filled his eyes and covered his rosy cheeks.

All the way the old woman had been muttering to herself in Spanish, but Paul could not understand that.

"I am so tired," he said, resting the basket upon the ground.

"Oh, it is not far! not far! and I will give you the bright crimson tuft—think of that," replied the old woman.

So Paul took up the basket, and again

they went on a long, long way, and turned
so many corners, he feared he could never
find his way back, but still the thought of
the crimson tuft allured him.

"I must have it," he said; "that would
be a real pleasure."

At last, when he was just ready to fall
down with fatigue, they came to a great
iron-barred gate, and the old woman rung
the bell very loudly.

In a moment a great rough voice called,
in Spanish, as through a trumpet, "Who
rings at the gate?"

Very soon the gate was opened by a
curious-looking dwarf, who started and
grinned fearfully when he saw Paul.

The child offered him the basket, but he
only shook his head, pointing after the old
woman, who gave him her staff, and walked
along with as much ease as little Paul
himself.

Now the child was really frightened, and would have run away, but he was already within the gate, and, with a great clang, it closed. The dwarf put up the iron bars, and replaced the bolts. Nothing could be more secure, for all around rose an immense high fence, topped with sharp spikes. It was impossible to escape—no one could get in or out.

A long avenue led to a pleasant-looking house, built in the Spanish fashion. It was shaded with beautiful trees, that had been brought from the southern country. How they waved their long fan-like leaves in the sunshine! It was a picture engraven upon the child's mind never to be effaced.

Under the shadow of the trees walked the old woman toward the house, and Paul followed with the basket, trembling like the light leaves of the tamarind. Just

behind him came the dwarf. He could
hear his heavy tread.

"It is no use! no use!" thought the
child; but he would gladly have given
the tempting crimson tuft, the red morocco
ball, all, all his pretty treasures, to have
been once more by the mother's side, sell-
ing vegetables in the market.

They entered a large, pleasant drawing-
room, with doors opening upon the front
piazza and upon the verandah of the inner
court, so that, though it was very warm, a
delicious breeze swept through the room,
and made it delightfully cool.

The old woman threw herself upon a
couch, and, pointing to a silver bell, told
Paul to ring it, adding, "My little cup-
bearer, you must be tired, and I will order
something to refresh you before you return
to your good mother."

"I am not so very tired," said Paul;

" let me go—the mother will need me;"
and he looked imploringly into the pitiless
face that he was beginning to fear above
all things.

" Ring the bell, boy," was the only
answer.

So he rang the bell, and the dwarf,
who had left them on the piazza, entered.

The woman addressed him in Spanish,
which Paul did not understand, but, as he
went to and from a large closet, and began
spreading the table, he would turn his
curious squinting eyes upon the child with
looks of compassion.

In a short time all was ready; and what
a delicious lunch it might have been to
the child, but for the great fear that over-
shadowed him ! Delicate cakes and confec-
tions, cold chicken, eggs, and all kinds of
fruits that children are so fond of, with

many nice-looking things that Paul had never seen before.

There was a great pyramid of ice-cream. "How I should like to eat it with the dear mother!" thought Paul.

Oh! that *was* a delicious lunch, to be sure!

"Come, let us sit down," said the old woman.

"I am not hungry," answered Paul, timidly; for he longed so greatly to be at home, that even these unaccustomed delicacies, and the promised crimson tuft, were as nothing compared with the sweet comfort at the dear mother's side.

"You silly child! You have walked all this distance, carrying that great basket, and are not hungry? Well, you are thirsty, and for your nectar of the gods, I will return you the sherbet of an eastern prince."

The woman filled a glass with a clear,

rosy liquid, that bubbled up and sparkled so temptingly, that little Paul, who was quite overcome with fatigue and thirst, grasped it eagerly, and did not take the glass from his lips till he had drained it to the bottom.

Then he wished to start for home, but he felt so drowsy that he could not move. He thought of the mother, but felt no emotion, and looked at the hideous old woman, who was grinning horribly, without fear. In a few moments he sunk down upon the couch, in a heavy sleep.

The woman stood over him, chuckling in great glee. "I have you now, my pretty cup-bearer, and will make you of great use to me. I will teach you a thousand things you would be glad not to know! You shall have a crimson tuft, ha! ha! ha! I will teach you to be impertinent to me! My hooked nose! to be sure. Ah! I am

old! old! and nothing can make me young
and fair. If I could only take for myself
your young beauty! But, no! one day I
must die, and that will be the end."

The woman's face grew convulsed—for
she was haunted by the grim specter, Death,
as with a dread terror. Her life had
been so filled with darkness, that she could
not look forward to the calm hereafter.
All the brightness and beauty of heaven,
the golden, was like the fleeting dreams
of childhood, that the rolling years, bear-
ing her to the portals of dim old age, had
swept away.

She had studied magic, and tried to find
the elixir of life, but in vain. She had
discovered many wonderful things, but not
the fountain of perpetual youth, nor the
precious elixir of life.

For a few moments she stood gazing at
the fresh face and rich curls of the child,

as he lay sleeping in his pure innocence. Once the word "mother" passed his rosy lips, and the woman waved a perfumed fan over him, till even the mother was no longer the companion of his dreamless sleep.

" Now, it will do to begin," said the old woman, and she took from a secret drawer in the closet several bottles containing liquids, and placed them on a little table. Taking a pair of sharp scissors, she sat down by the child, and cut off all his beautiful brown curls, leaving only a little tuft. This she made quite stiff in some way, and colored it bright red, tying it upon the top of his head, so that it stood up and looked very strangely.

" There is the crimson tuft, my little cup-bearer," she said, laughing heartily at her wicked work.

Then she tinged his eyebrows red, and

his skin a dark mahogany color, until, instead of the beautiful little Paul that everybody had loved and admired, he appeared the ugliest little wretch one could well imagine.

She took off his neat, plain clothes, dressing him in yellow leather breeches and a fantastic red jacket. Upon his feet she put shoes with long pointed toes, that turned up and were tied with red ribbons. When she had finished, she looked at him with great satisfaction.

"Even the old dame herself would not know her cub now. What an ugly little goat he has become, to be sure!" And the old woman, after her usual way, muttered to herself.

At last she sat down, and, eating and drinking, for, by this time, she was quite hungry, every few moments she would stop and rub her long bony hands together. and laugh, as she looked at the transformed child.

Paul slept all the afternoon, and awoke in the dusky shadow of the twilight, confused and bewildered, to find himself in a strange room with the horrible woman, sitting before a blazing fire. gazing steadily into its fantastic pictures.

At first he could not tell where he was, but in a moment he remembered all, and jumped up in the greatest excitement, saying, "How could I have slept, when the dear mother was expecting me? She will be so anxious. Oh, let me go to her! Please, good lady, let me go!"

"What do you mean," answered the old woman. "You have no mother! you are my little servant, Crimson Tuft. I gave you that name, myself, on account of your red hair, which stands up like a crest on the top of your ugly head."

Then the child began to cry, saying, "My hair is not red, and my name is Paul, and it was my dear mother who sold you vegetables at the market this morning. Let me go home, oh! please let me go home to the dear mother."

The child's voice was broken with sobs, but the hard-hearted woman only laughed, "Ha! ha! it is a curious dream you have had, or are you going crazy? your hair not red! indeed! why, look in the glass yourself."

She led him to a mirror, and there the unhappy child saw reflected the ugly wretch called Crimson Tuft, but never again the handsome little Paul.

The child was more frightened and bewildered than ever. He was sure he had left the mother that morning, in company with this horrible old woman. Every thing in the rude little home rose in his mind, yet he could not realize his own identity. Paul surely he could not see in the reflecting mirror, only the ugly little Crimson Tuft.

He raised his hands and took hold of the stiff shock of red hair that stood upright upon his head. Oh, no! it was not Paul's soft silken curls.

Yet there *was a look* about the eyes that reminded him of Paul, but even they were very different: they were the red, swollen, terror-strained eyes of Crimson Tuft.

"Are you satisfied now," said the old woman. "It was only a dream, a queer dream that you have had, Crimson Tuft, and how funny that you should think you were an old vegetable-woman's child. You, my servant, who have never been out of this place in your life."

Still the child only cried the more, and

entreated, " Let me go home to the mother,
let me go home."

Though he was faint from the effects of
the narcotic, and from fasting for a long
time, he refused food, and continued to sob,
begging the old woman to let him go home,
but she only answered, " you are dreaming
still, or crazy." Then she told him how
sometimes people were bewitched, and did
not know themselves.

" Still, I am Paul, let me go." At last
the woman, losing all patience, called the
dwarf to beat him, if he did not stop crying and begin to eat. So terror and hunger at last conquered, and the little boy,
choking down his sobs, sat upon a stool in
silence, to eat his supper, very desolate and
leaden hearted.

From that day a new era commenced
in the history of the child. An era of
servitude, sorrow, and tears, that washed

away so far into the past the memory of his free and joyous childhood, that he began to believe what the woman so often told him, that his mind had gone astray, that he had been bewitched.

Sometimes he would stand looking long into the great mirror, at the stiff, red hairs and brown skin of poor Crimson Tuft, thinking what a beautiful myth it was, about the happy little Paul, and the dear mother. How it had stolen into his heart like a real life, and still the señora, as all about the house called her, said it was only a bewildering dream.

Into his eyes he would often look, saying, "Those are Paul's eyes, but the red brows give a different expression to their sadness," he would add, "No! no! they are not Paul's eyes."

Always the red hair, brown skin and sorrowful heart, "I must be only poor Crimson Tuft."

Very often his hungry heart would cry out, "Oh, mother! mother!"

Too often the shrill voice of the old woman would be the discordant answer, sending him to some new task.

As months, then years, rolled by, the child became more accustomed to his sorrowful lot, and in many ways it grew pleasanter. He learned to talk Spanish fluently, and became very fond of the queer looking dwarf, who had frightened him so much at first. He often talked to him about his mysterious change, but of these things the dwarf would never speak, so at last Crimson Tuft ceased to mention them.

His kind-hearted friend taught him many things in leisure hours—to read, write, and solve difficult problems—so that

8*

at twelve, he was as much advanced in his studies as most boys of his age.

With the señora he had become quite a favorite, although at first, for a long time, he had only menial service to perform, there came a change. One day she heard him reading aloud to the dwarf, and was so much delighted with his distinct enunciation, and fine rendition of what happened to be a favorite author, that she called him to her private library, and talked a long time in a way she had never before addressed him.

"He is a boy of quick mind," thought she, "and may be more than an ordinary servant to me. He is just what I shall need in my troublesome Mexican affairs. I must train him to his work."

From that day he used to sit hours in the library reading to her, and often she gave him long papers to copy, which he was soon able to do, to her entire satisfaction.

Very often she would talk to him as though he were a man, in fact the training he was receiving brought only the man's thoughts. He had left his happy boyhood at the little stall in the market-place.

One day he found an old guitar in the attic of an out-house, which was filled with broken furniture, and many things disused and forgotten. From that hour he enjoyed a real pleasure. In a short time he picked out the chords and wove them into delicious harmonies, and then there came into his mind a rich old melody of the fatherland. It was like the memory of a happy dream, and the tears filled his eyes. Again he was happy, for every thing save the spell of the divine melody was forgotten.

Two more years glided by, and the young boy was advancing toward man-

hood. He was tall, and finely developed;
and deep within his dreamy eyes slept the
wonderful magnetic charm. Still the
brown skin and stiff hair remained, and he
was only poor ugly Crimson Tuft.

In all this time he had never been outside the massive gate which was always
strongly locked and barred; and though he
had often entreated the dwarf, the only
reply was a grave shake of the head, and
a sad, compassionate look, from the odd
squinting eyes of his companion, and if he
persisted the dwarf would go away and
leave him alone.

He had never ventured to speak to the
Señora but once, on the subject, in years,
and then her fury was so unbounded, that
he feared she would tear him in pieces with
her long bony fingers, which, when she was
enraged, possessed the power of a vice.
For a week after, she fed him on bread and

water, and kept him confined in a dark
room with too heavy tasks to allow him
to question the mysterious past, or specu-
late on the uncertain future.

"Always a foolish dreamer," she said. "I
will teach you something, you, the brown-
skinned Crimson Tuft."

Yet it was all no use: the boy had his
thoughts, that could not be chained. He
was determined to escape.

"I will not excite suspicion; I will strive
to please; and a time will come, yes, the
time will come, when I shall know all."

Thus in striving to lull the suspicions of
the Argus-eyed woman to sleep, he grew
into great favor, and became indispensable
to her.

"He can do so many things that no one
else can do," she would say to herself, "but
those great luminous eyes torment me. If
they too could be changed. But that is

beyond my power. Would I could make them dull leaden, and red as his flaming crimson tuft. He is useful, very useful, but there are times, with all his quiet seem-ing, when I think he suspects me. Dare I trust him ? that is the question."

Here the old woman would fall into long fits of musing, and gaze into the glowing embers, till they faded into dead ashes.

One morning the old woman called Crim-son Tuft to her, saying : "I am going away, to be gone for some days, and I want you to copy these papers for me. They are the deeds and other valuable papers of my property in Mexico, which you will see is very great. Let the copies be made with great distinctness, for these duplicates may be required. You see I am cautious, and trust you very much, very much."

A look of suspicion crossed her sharp wizen face; but in the ugly brown countenance she could detect nothing but truth and sincerity.

"I can do no better," she thought, but aloud she added, " the dwarf knows all and will see to the safety of these and every thing. If one of them is lost it would bring no end of trouble, and you would have your share." With an ominous shake of the head, the old señora rose and left Crimson Tuft bending over the yellowed parchment, that was of the most inestimable value to her.

About noon she left the house, with the dwarf following her to the gate, which, when she had passed he barred more securely than ever.

For some days Crimson Tuft worked diligently over the papers. There were deeds of haciendas and mines, mortgages, and grants of land, and many long, intricate pages of law papers. Really to copy all

these was a task, and Crimson Tuft was
filled with amazement at the greatness of
the old señora's possessions.

At last they were all finished, and locked
up by the dwarf in the iron-bound oaken
chest, and that again was locked in the
great closet, and the dwarf carried the key.
So it was very secure.

Still the old señora did not return!
"Now the time has come," thought Crimson Tuft, "I must escape." But that was
easier planned than done. Everywhere the
dwarf followed him, and when Crimson
Tuft grew angry he laid his heavy hand
upon his arm, saying, "from the first I
have loved you, boy,—believe me it will all
be well—only wait a little longer."

Then Crimson Tuft took his hard, honest
hand, saying, "you alone have loved me,
and for your sake I will wait, but not long,
I *can not*—do not ask it."

One evening, about a week after this, the bell rang, and the señora entered, followed by a most beautiful little maiden about twelve years of age.

She was dressed in mourning, with a black shawl about her head; her long glossy hair hung carelessly over her graceful shoulders; her complexion was a clear olive, and her skin soft and smooth as satin; while her large, dark eyes had a depth as of the mystic sea, and a pure clear look as of heaven.

They were more beautiful than anything Crimson Tuft had ever seen, and some how they startled him. It was not like the old vision, yet it touched him more deeply—this was of the present—that of the past.

"This is my only granddaughter," said the old woman to the dwarf and Crimson Tuft. Both bowed very low to the pretty señorita. They were such a queer-looking pair, that she clapped her dainty little hands together laughing in a pure ring ing tone, clear as the notes of a silver bell.

Poor Crimson Tuft was very much con-fused, for to him the young Donna Leota was the first dream of beauty that had kindled the dawning fire of manhood in his heart, and he was ready to bow down and kiss her foot-prints in the sand.

Strange to say, the little Leota swayed the grandmother as absolutely as she had ruled the dwarf and Crimson Tuft, but in one respect the old woman was resolute, the heavy gate was locked as securely upon Leota as upon the other inmates of the mansion, and no persuasion could induce her to change in this regard.

Leota was passionately fond of music, and played the harp very sweetly.

Once in the still hours of night, she was

awakened by the notes of her own harp vibrating in the most exquisite harmony.

She was filled with delight though she trembled with fear, for she was quite sure there was no one in the house who knew any thing of music but herself, yet the chords were swept as by a master's hand.

She lay motionless until the last note died away, and it was long before she fell asleep, for the spell of the rich melodies still floated through the air around her. In the morning she spoke of it, but no one could explain the mystery. Again and again, in the silent hours came the rich melody, not old familiar airs, but the exquisite improvisations of genius.

One night, when the golden moon was casting its soft amber light over land and sea, and the enchanted harp sending forth its entrancing strains, Leota rose softly from her couch, and summoning all her courage, determined herself to solve the mystery. She glided quietly along the passage-way to the large glass door of the parlor, and there she saw Crimson Tuft bending fondly over the harp, and calling out the bewildering melody that she had thought could be born only of mystical enchantment. The imagination of the young girl was so vivid that she was easily prepared for things supernatural, but to see poor brown Crimson Tuft, the great magician, he, the slave, of whom she thought only to laugh at—this was stranger than all.

The soft moonlight fell full upon his face, and his large luminous eyes were dewy with the spirit of the rich melody. With the rare beauty that was all their own, they almost redeemed the brown skin and flaming hair from positive ugliness. Leota stood entranced till the last note

died out of the thrilled chords of the
trembling harp, then, as she turned to go,
the rustling of her robe caused Crimson
Tuft to raise his eyes, and they fell full
upon her face, to him at least the most
beautiful face in the world. He was
covered with deep confusion. Over his
redeeming eyes fell the heavy red lashes,
and the ugly brows contracted.

She, his rare divinity, had seen him play,
and heard how the notes flowed from his
own heart, through the sympathizing
harp-strings that thrilled with his devotion to her, which would last all his life
long.

Leota was greatly bewildered, and as
she stole away to her own room, strange
thoughts chased themselves through her
mind. Not one word had been spoken,
but every thing had changed. Crimson
Tuft was no longer only the ugly servant

of her grandmother, but he was Crimson
Tuft of the mystery.

There was something interesting in that;
besides, shut up in those high walls, with
only the old grandmother for company,
and little amusement, one must think a
great deal. So Leota had her thoughts.
Crimson Tuft had wonderful eyes. She
had found that out, and it was a great
deal there in that dull place.

She wished to be in Mexico again, where
the most beautiful flowers bloom, and the
delicious fruit grows ripe on the broad-
leafed trees. Yet she did not like to think
she would never see the beautiful eyes
again. "But one must not think too
much of a servant," she would say to herself. "She was of good blood, and that
 ould not do, yet one must treat inferiors
ƙindly." Really it was difficult to tell
what one must do. So, all in a maze, she

fell asleep, and dreamed of the most radiant eyes, which *were* Crimson Tuft's, and the handsomest face, which surely *was not* Crimson Tuft's.

The morning dawned clear and bright, as Crimson Tuft arose and began the duties of the day. Though he was advanced to the post of private secretary, the old señora had left him some tasks in the early part of the day that would prevent him from forgetting his position as a servant.

First he swept and dusted the parlor and halls. This had always been his work, and no one else could please the señora so well. As he dusted the señorita's harp a flash of indignation filled his heart. He was only a servant, the ugly Crimson Tuft, and she the most beautiful maiden, the divinity of his soul. There was a great difference, yet he felt himself a man, and

he would conquer fate in the end, even
with his ugly Crimson Tuft. This was
what he thought.

When Leota appeared she said nothing
of her discovery, but when she spoke to
him it was in a different tone from for-
merly. The mystery of the enchanted harp
was over, but the greater mystery had
begun.

The wonderful eyes acted as a talisman upon her heart, and though she strove
against it, she found herself forgetting
Crimson Tuft's position, his ugly brown
skin and red hair.

One glance of his beaming eyes would
set her warm blood dancing through her
veins till her neck and brow were a soft
rose-tint, and this was in no way pleasant
to the proud little maiden.

The next night Crimson Tuft did not
touch the harp, and in the morning the

Donna Leota passed him at his work with a haughty toss of her dainty head, but with a quiver in her voice she said, " Crimson Tuft, play when you like, the music pleases me."

After that Crimson Tuft would always play at twilight, and even the old grand-mother was touched by the magical spell of his genius.

Every year the old woman grew more infirm, till she could not even walk from room to room without leaning upon her staff. At times her temper was terrible, and nothing but the soft touch of Leota's hand could calm her. She loved with all her strong hard nature the young maiden who daily was growing to womanhood crowned with surpassing beauty.

She was getting very old. With an iron will she resisted the pitiless hand of time, but she could not stay it. Her long hands became more bony and angular, her

9

eyes more red and bleared, and her voice more cracked and shrill; yet she seemed to be looking forward to a long life, and was more hard and grasping than ever. It was only Leota that she loved more than gold.

One night Crimson Tuft had a curious dream. He thought, as he lay half sleeping and half waking, dreaming delightful but impossible things, that the old woman came in softly and poured something upon his head, and that when he started, she held a sponge to his nose, until he sank back powerless. He seemed to inhale something sweet and fragrant. It was very pleasant and soothing: that was all he could remember. In the morning, he felt heavy and drowsy, his head ached, but he roused himself, rose and dressed as usual. When he looked in the glass he saw that his hair was redder, and his skin a deeper brown than ever. Memories and a strange suspicion flashed over his mind.

Far back in the years he remembered dimly a little boy, named Paul, a fair child, whom he had been taught to believe a dream. There was a mystery. Could she have changed Paul to Crimson Tuft in a night?

After this, Crimson Tuft became more thoughtful than ever. There was a mystery to solve, and he would devote all his energies to it. He was eighteen years old, a very intelligent young man, but entirely unacquainted with the world. He had yet much to learn.

One day the old woman called him to her, and looked, in her curious way, at him for a long time. "Crimson Tuft," she said, "you are my servant, but I have given you great advantages, so that you are as well educated as many a rich man's

son. But that is not all; I wish to make
your fortune."

Then the old woman fell into a deep
study, and Crimson Tuft stood waiting
and wondering what would come next.

At length he grew tired. "Señora," he
said, "you wanted to speak with me."

She gave a sudden start as he spoke.
"Oh! yes," she replied, "but I had forgotten you. You are my servant, and have
been so always."

"Always?" asked Crimson Tuft.

A dark frown passed over the old woman's face, and Crimson Tuft regretted his
folly. He was very anxious to hear what
she had to say to him. There might be
some hope of relief. But again she was
silent; and, worse than all, she seemed
displeased.

The Donna Leota passed the open window, singing lightly a pretty Spanish air,

and the shadows began to clear away from the clouded brow.

" Excuse me, señora," said Crimson Tuft, softly. " If in some way I can serve you, I shall be only too happy." He, too, had heard the soothing song.

" Crimson Tuft," she replied, " I am not now so strong as I was twenty good years ago, and I want some one near me whom I can trust, for I have affairs that must be attended to now—some one who will not cheat me out of my gold. I have looked carefully about, and can see no one but you—you, whom I have trained, educated, and cared for so many years. The world is so ungrateful and wicked! Even you, who owe every thing to me, might rob me— me, an old woman. It would be a wicked thing—a great crime !"

The red, eager eyes of the old woman were fastened upon the face of the young man, and with all her shrewdness she tried to read him. Her pinched features grew sharper, and her voice shrill as the whistling wind. She grasped her staff, and hobbled across the room several times, in an excited manner.

"You are such a curious, ugly fellow. What have *you* to hope for in the world, save from me? But, if you are faithful, I will advance you. But I can as easily punish as reward."

The red blood flushed even the brown cheek of the boy, for he was painfully conscious of his extreme ugliness, and he thought sadly of the Donna Leota.

"Listen, boy," continued the old woman. "There is a great world beyond these walls. Can I trust you to go away over the waters with me? Remember all I promise you, and be faithful."

She looked steadfastly into the luminous

eyes of Crimson Tuft, that dilated with pleasurable exultation. She was evidently satisfied with the truth and sincerity she saw beaming there, for she proceeded :—

"I must go again to Mexico, but not alone. The Donna Leota will accompany me, for in the years to come I can not be separated from her. And you must go, as I shall need you. I am very rich, and must trust you with a great secret; but I have studied you well."

"Señora," said Crimson Tuft, eagerly, "I will be true to you; you shall never regret."

"Swear it!" she said, fiercely.

So the young boy knelt, and pressed the good book to his lips, repeating after her a most solemn oath, to serve her faithfully, and keep sacred the great secret, which was to be revealed to Leota only, in case of the grandmother's death.

"Now," she said, "I am weary. To-morrow I will tell you all." And she leaned back in the arm-chair, and shaded her eyes with her fan. Crimson Tuft went out, with his heart beating wild in a tumult of conflicting emotions.

On the morrow, again she called him to the library, and locked the door.

"I have made my will," she said, "and you are handsomely provided for, in consideration of your proving faithful to the trust I repose in you. Besides this, while I live, you shall never want for gold. Is it all fully understood?" ·

Then Crimson Tuft said, " It is understood, señora, fully." And she took from her desk a carefully sealed paper, which she wrapped in sheep-skin, and, again sealing it, gave it to the boy. "This paper," she said, "describes the exact spot where a great treasure is hidden upon my hacienda,

near the City of Mexico. There is no
chance of your gaining this for yourself,
for there are two other persons living who
have similar papers; indeed, precautions,
that I shall not tell you of, have been
taken, so that it must fall to the Donna
Leota at last, for she is the only true
heiress. You see I am cautious, very cautious," she added, the old look of suspicion
rising in her face.

From this day Crimson Tuft was her
chief adviser. He and the dwarf made
all preparations for the journey. In about
a week all was ready, and they went to
San Francisco in a carriage, which drove
immediately down to the steamer, and they
were soon comfortably settled on board.

" Now," said Crimson Tuft, " there is
still time, and I can walk about the city
for half an hour." But the señora grew
excited, and exclaimed, " No! no! you

9*

might get lost; remember, you are a
stranger." And the Donna Leota said,
softly, "Surely, you will not go away!"

So the dwarf performed all the commis-
sions, and for an hour the señora was ab-
sent; but, before leaving, she had said to
Crimson Tuft, "I leave the Donna Leota in
your care."

At length the ship sailed. Then came
the long, sluggish, dreamy days at sea.
Crimson Tuft and Leota were often together upon the deck, for the old señora
would not allow her there alone. What gold-
en days they were to the poor Crimson Tuft.
More and more he was growing to love the
pretty young señorita, and she could not resist the powerful spell of his luminous eyes.

One night she rushed wildly through
the saloon to his state-room. The grandmother had been taken suddenly very ill,
and must see Crimson Tuft.

She breathed with great difficulty, and her words came low and broken: "If I live to reach Mexico, you will not need this paper; but I am old," she added, bitterly, "and the old must die."

With great pain she went on: "If I should not live to reach the hacienda, you will see the child has her own. Dig up the treasure yourself, and do not defraud her of one single gold piece, or the curse of a dying woman will follow you, even from the darkness of the grave." Then again Crimson Tuft promised, and, taking the paper, left her alone with "the child," as she still fondly called the Donna Leota.

This attack passed away, but another soon followed, and again Crimson Tuft was summoned to her side. Her glazed eye brightened as she saw him. "Remember," was all she could say, and again he made the solemn promise. It was the third and

last time. With the old señora all was
now over.

Leota trembled with fear, and wept bitterly. The grandmother had loved her, and
now there was no one left, only Crimson
Tuft, who sat by her side all through the
silent hours.

The next evening, at sunset, the old
señora was buried in the sea.

No one wept but the beautiful young
maiden, as the steamer went on, leaving in
its wake the cold, lifeless body, wrapped in
its shroud of sparkling waters.

At length the good ship arrived safely
in Mexico, and Crimson Tuft took the proud
young heiress to the hacienda, where a
crowd of friends and retainers awaited her.

The will was opened, and there was a
large legacy left to Crimson Tuft. But it was
as nothing to him. With so much ugliness,
what had he to hope for!

In the last paper the señora had handed him, there was a still fuller description of the spot where the treasure was hidden, and a night appointed for him to seek it. It was the eighteenth birthnight of the Donna Leota. Till then, she was to be placed in a convent, and Crimson Tuft was to have the best tutors in the City of Mexico. This would make a man of him.

So the young people were separated for a time, but the two years soon rolled by, and Crimson Tuft returned to the hacienda with his papers.

What a change there was in him. His brown, dark face had grown every day more fair, and his stiff red hair more soft and silky, and of a rich brown color. It was really wonderful. The young man was transformed, day by day, from the ugly Crimson Tuft to the handsome Paul.

The Donna Leota had become the beautiful woman that her childhood promised, and when she met Paul after the two years of separation, she felt that the great mystery was solved, and knew that she could never love any one else. So they were betrothed, and she was to be made his wife on her eighteenth birthday.

At the appointed time, Paul sought and found the great treasure that had been hidden for so long. There were immense iron pots, full of shining gold pieces, that had been hidden during one of the many Mexican revolutions. Thus it was found that the Donna Leota was the richest maiden in all Mexico, and she had many suitors among the wealthy Spanish hidalgoes; but she cared only for Paul, for the spell of the wonderful eyes, which had been Crimson Tuft's, was upon her.

At last, the joyous wedding-day came, and every one said, "What a tall, handsome señor is the bridegroom, and how very lovely the bride. The sun shines upon them and it will be a happy marriage."

Soon after, they went to San Francisco, and Paul felt the old dream returning.

One day, as he walked through the market-place, he came to a vegetable stand. Behind it sat a sorrowful woman, with a sad, mild face, that woke the sleeping memories of his heart. "Mother!" he exclaimed, with a thrill of tenderness in his voice that raised the bowed head of the lonely one. She gave one look into the eyes that, once seen, could never be forgotten, and cried, "Paul! my son, my son!" and opening her arms, received upon her bosom the head of her long lost treasure.

How she wept, and smiled, and pressed him to her heart; then held him off, that she might gaze upon the dear handsome face.

Then they went home to the father, who

was old and sick. He had lost strength and heart years ago, and they were very poor. "He has never held up his head," so the mother said, "since our boy was taken from us."

But that was all over; the lost was found; poverty, sorrow, and sickness fled with his presence.

He took the old father and mother home to Leota, who received them into her own heart; for, were they not his parents and hers?

At first the old vegetable woman stood a little in awe of her high-born daughter, but that soon melted away in the warmth of the dainty little Señora's affection; and the father, mother, son, and daughter, lived all their lives together, a happy family, united in heart and mind by the silken bonds of a true, earnest affection.

SNOWDROP AND ROSEBUD.

A CALIFORNIA STORY.

YEARS ago, before the gold-seekers came to California, there lived at the Mission of San Gabriel, a Spaniard, whose beautiful vineyard was admired by all the country.

In early life he had been a great traveler, and while in Germany, he met a fair golden-haired maiden, whom he loved and married. After a few years he emigrated to America, and settled at the Mission of San Gabriel—near the town of Los Angeles.

There he prospered greatly, his cattle increased to great herds, covering the green hill-sides, and his vineyard was the pride of his heart. He built a pleasant house, and surrounded it with a garden filled

with all kinds of fruit. In that delicious
climate, fruits of the tropic and temperate
zones grow together; while the white
flowers of the North, and their crimson-hued
sisters of the South, blossom side by side.

There seemed nothing wanting to make
his happiness complete but children. The
house was too silent; he wished for the
silvery laughter of childish voices; he
longed to press little ones to his heart, and
call them his own.

At last, God gave him two little girls;
but the fair, golden-haired mother lived
only to bless them, and was then buried by
the clear " Lake of the Tulés." At first he
was inconsolable, and for months refused
to see his little ones; but one day, while he
slept, the old Indian nurse took them into
his room, and laid them on the bed by his
side.

Little Snowdrop nestled in his bosom,

but Rosebud ran her fingers into his beard, and pulled it so hard that she woke him. There she was, when he opened his eyes, crowing with delight—her little rosy lips close to his, and the fair Snowdrop in his bosom.

Then all the father's love, which had only slept, awoke, and he pressed the little ones to his heart, weeping; but especially he loved the beautiful Snowdrop, she was so like her mother.

After this, although he still mourned greatly for his wife, he loved these little ones very dearly; and as years passed by, became happy in the absorbing devotion to them, which filled his whole heart.

He watched over them with the most jealous care. Even in childhood, he would not allow them to play with other children; and as they grew older, his fear was awakened lest some of the young señors of Los Angeles should see and fall in love with them. For his daughters to form a mésalliance, he was quite sure would break his heart.

As he was obliged often to go from home on business, he employed an old Indian woman as duenna, and charged her never to allow the girls out of her sight for a moment.

Rosebud was a Spanish girl, with purple-tinged hair, soft black eyes, and clear olive complexion. Through the satin skin the warm blood flushed her cheeks, and her lips were more tempting than ripe cherries; but Snowdrop was a rare German maiden in complexion, clear and fair as the noonday. Her eyes were like violets. Her hair in the sunshine was like fine spun gold, and so long that it reached to her feet, and hung like a mantle of glory about her.

It was no wonder the old man guarded his daughters so carefully; for though so different, they were equally beautiful, and all the young men of good family were anxious to pay court to them.

Day by day they sat upon the piazza of the inner court, reading the fascinating romances of old Spain, which was to them the dreamland of delight. They longed very much to go out, and see something of life among the rich Spanish families about San Gabriel and Los Angeles, but their father would not allow it; and the old duenna was always near them; even when they walked through the vineyard or the orange orchard, she followed them.

One day, Rosebud called Snowdrop into the garden, and sitting under a large almond-tree, she said : "Look over this book of prints with me, while we talk softly, for the duenna must not hear every thing."

Snowdrop rested her golden tresses upon her sister's arm, and, turning over the leaves of the book, they talked together.

"Sister dear," said Rosebud, "we lead a very dull life here. All young girls are gay and happy. What is the use of being beautiful, with no one to see us but servants and old women?" A look of conscious beauty gathered around her pouting lips, as she ran her dainty fingers through the silken meshes of her sister's golden hair.

"Our dear papa loves us," said Snowdrop, "but I do wish to be loved by others," she added—her violet eyes softening, and a faint flush spreading over her fair cheeks and neck.

"And I to be admired! but how can we be either?" replied Rosebud, "shut up here, with the old duenna to watch every thing we do? God made us beautiful, and I'm sure he intended us to be seen. And for my part, I am determined to go to the consul's grand ball, if I have to run away!" and her pretty dark eyes filled with tears.

"Oh! sister Rosebud, think of the dear papa!" said Snowdrop.

"He did not tell us not to go out of the garden alone; he only told the duenna to watch us. If we could only manage her," said Rosebud, thoughtfully.

"I am afraid it would not be right," replied Snowdrop, "but I want to go very much. We will make an altar-cloth, and embroider it with gold, as an offering to the Blessed Virgin. Perhaps she will pity our loneliness, and help us."

So they wrought an altar cloth of purple and gold, and spread it upon the altar, before the picture of the Blessed Mother, in their own chamber; putting vases of beautiful flowers upon it. When it was finished they were quite happy, and sat down with their guitars, and sang very sweetly together, till their father came home.

The next moring, an old Mexican woman, with baskets of trinkets for sale, knocked at the garden gate.

When she was admitted, she spread out her finery before the young señoritas. The duenna hastened to the piazza where they were sitting—for no one was more fond of looking over the *vendedora's* basket than she, always finding something she could not do without among its tempting stores —this time it was a gay-colored shawl, and she ran away for her purse.

As soon as she was out of sight, the old woman whispered:—

"Pretty señoritas, I have charms to sell. This will make you admired, and this

loved," she said, holding up two curious
little bags—one tied with long pink ribbon, the other with blue—"and this,"
pointing to a third, " will make you sleep.
It contains a powder. You must drop one
grain into a glass of water. It is perfectly
tasteless, but it brings on a sleep so pro-
found, that until the effect passes away,
nothing could awaken you from pleasant
dreams."

The young girls bought the charms.
Snowdrop took the one tied with blue ribbon, and placing it in her bosom, whispered, " Now I may be loved."

" And I will be admired," said Rosebud,
taking the other; but the charm for sleep
she concealed in her pocket, just as the
old duenna returned, eager for her purchases.

" I have pretty slippers for little dancing
feet," said the old woman, holding up two

pairs of the daintiest white satin slippers
you could imagine.

"The señoritas have no use for them,"
exclaimed the duenna, frowning; but the
young girls found that they fitted so nicely,
and looked so pretty, they bought them.

"Papa is rich enough to give us any
thing we want, and we fancy these," said
Rosebud. They bought strings of beads,
ribbons, and combs for their hair, until the
old duenna was nearly frantic. What
they could want of all these, shut up as
they were, she could not tell.

Then Rosebud said:—"We will have
some new dresses;" so they bought fine
white muslin and lace. Snowdrop bought
a bright-colored handkerchief, which she
gave the duenna, who was so much pleased
that she promised to help them make their
dresses.

As soon as the old woman went away,

they all sat upon the piazza, shaded with vines, and commenced cutting and stitching upon the delicate fabric so busily, that by evening the skirts of their dresses were quite finished.

The next morning they were early at work again.

"Why do you hurry so much," said the duenna, who never liked to work very long at a time.

"To have it over the sooner, dear duenna," answered Snowdrop, smiling so sweetly that the duenna took her needle again quite pleasantly.

Snowdrop's dress was trimmed with blue ribbon, Rosebud's with crimson and gold. The young girls wrought upon them all their pretty fancies, till, when they were finished, the duenna thought them beautiful enough for a queen.

At evening the work was all done; and

the duenna, quite fatigued with her unaccustomed task, sat dozing in her armchair.

Suddenly she roused herself, exclaiming :—" How warm it is ! I am very thirsty."

" Rosebud jumped up quickly, saying, "I will bring you fresh water;" so she ran down to the spring at the foot of the garden, and there she met the faithful old Miguel—who had been in the family for years before she was born, and loved the young señoritas as though they were his own children.

Rosebud caught him by the arm, and whispered :—" Have the horses at the back garden-gate to-night at nine o'clock, you dear old Miguel, for you shall take us to the consul's ball."

"But the señor?" said the old servant, in astonishment.

"Never mind the señor, you dear, careful man."

"But the duenna?" he continued.

"Never mind! never mind! I tell you I will go! so be sure you are ready in time," said Rosebud, laughing, and shaking her finger as she ran away.

Poor old Miguel was in a great dilemma. He loved the pretty señoritas, and wanted to help them; but he feared the señor.

"It may cost me my place; and in this family I have lived, and here I would die; but my pretty children are so lonely, it is too bad to shut them up—and old Miguel will not fail them."

Thus his fond love for the fair girls he had carried in his arms in their helpless infancy, conquered his discretion; and he went to the stable to groom the horses.

Rosebud brought the water—clear, cool, and sparkling—to the old duenna, and she

drank it eagerly in her thirst, little dreaming of the sleep-charm the gay young señorita had dropped into the cup.

Almost instantly she became very drowsy, and, closing her eyes, she fell asleep in
her chair. In a short time her heavy
breathing told how surely the charm had
taken effect.

"Now for the ball!" said Rosebud. So
the young girls dressed themselves quickly,
but with great care—looping their sleeves
with rare flowers from the garden, and
tying their ribbons very tastefully.

"I think we shall do," said Rosebud,
looking at the beautiful girl reflected from
her mirror, then at the softer beauty of her
sister.

Snowdrop answered by a kiss, and they
went out softly, and down the garden path
to the gate, where the faithful Miguel wait-
ed for them.

An hour's ride brought them to the brilliantly lighted mansion of the consul, and all the young señors were delighted at the arrival of the fair sisters.

No one was so much courted and admired, among all the fair señoritas at the ball that night, as Snowdrop and Rosebud; and none of the gay hidalgoes were more happy than old Miguel, who was peeping from behind the hall door, enjoying the triumph of his darlings. At last he became uneasy, and, approaching them with a respectful bow, told them it was time to go home.

Taking special leave of their host and hostess, bowing gracefully to the guests, they started for home—leaving all, admirers, and many, lovers behind them.

When they entered their chamber, they found the duenna still sleeping soundly. They undressed themselves noiselessly, put-

ting away all their clothes but their slippers, which they forgot.

In the morning, when the sun arose, the
duenna awoke, and was much surprised to
find herself sitting in a chair, instead of
being in bed.

She had but a confused recollection of
things, and began to think she must have
taken a little more wine than she intended
at dinner the day before. She thought she
remembered Rosebud giving her a glass
of water when she was very thirsty, but
she was not sure that it might not have
been wine.

She looked around, but could discover
nothing to help her. The two girls were
sleeping soundly, and upon the face of
Rosebud there was a smile. She was
dreaming of the ball—again surrounded
by a crowd of admirers.

Snowdrop dreamed of the dear papa;

he was angry with them for their disobe-
dience, and her long eyelashes were wet
with tears.

" How different they are in their ways,
even in sleep !" said the duenna.

She turned away, and as her eye fell
upon the forgotten slippers, her search-
ing glance detected that they had been
worn.

" What does this mean ? So much worn,
and bought yesterday ! 'T is very strange !"
mused she, and put them in her pocket.

She woke the young girls, but they fell
asleep again. They were so unused to
dancing late at night, that they were very
tired ; and when the bell rang for breakfast, they did not appear.

" Where are my dear daughters ?" said
the father, with a clouded face.

She could only tell him that they were
still asleep, and seemed very tired.

10*

"So are my horses," replied he, angrily; "but I will see about this."

The duenna was afraid to show him the shoes, lest he should blame her; but in her confusion, as she drew her handkerchief from her pocket, one of them dropped out upon the floor.

"What is this?" said the señor, sternly; and she was obliged to tell him all she knew.

For some time the troubled father walked the floor with great agitation without speaking, while the duenna stood trembling before him. Then, turning to her quickly, he said:—

"Call my daughters;" and he rang the bell for Miguel.

All three came into the room with fearful hearts; but Snowdrop's face was covered with her golden hair, and the tears were shining through it.

Turning to Miguel, he said, sternly, with a black frown covering his whole face :—

"Stand here, and tell me how it is, that this morning I find my horses reeking with foam ?"

The old man only answered, " I alone am to blame, señor. Pardon your old servant, who loves you and yours!" and he clasped his hands, and looked imploringly at the dark, angry face that frowned upon him.

Then Snowdrop could bear it no longer, so she ran to the father—throwing her white arms around his neck, and resting her golden-crowned head upon his bosom, she said :—

" Dear papa, I will tell you all! Only do not blame dear, good old Miguel."

Then she told him of all their loneliness, and eager longings for companions of their own age ; about the altar-cloth and all,

without reserving one thing. "And now
we are sorry; it was wrong; but the dear
papa will forgive!" and she raised her
pretty face, all shining with tears, and
begged him to kiss her.

How like her mother she was! and the
father thought of the sunny days of his
youth, when he had wandered on the
banks of the Rhine with the fair German
maiden, and wondered how he could forget
that the young and ardent hearts of his
children must be like the heart of his
youth.

He kissed the innocent face upturned to
his, and forgave them, saying, " I, too, have
been to blame ; and, in future, I will go
with you to all places, my darlings, where
it is proper and right for you to go."

Snowdrop and Rosebud were delighted,
and willingly promised never again to de-
ceive "the dear papa;" and from that day

there was mutual confidence and love between the young girls and the father.

After a time, when two brave and gallant knights sought of the father the hands of the fair señoritas in marriage, he answered, "Let the hearts of my dear children decide for you. My only wish is to see them happy."

There was a great feast made at their marriage; and the old Spanish house, so long wrapped in seclusion, resounded with joyous music and the merry laughter of light hearts. Again old Miguel stood behind the door, and rejoiced to see his darlings loved, admired, and happy.

It was a dark rainy day in the land where the rain makes the winter, and the sunshine and blue sky the pleasant summer-time.

Through the Golden Gate, came the ship to the new city of hope, and all the people on board thought, " how happy and rich we shall become in the Gold Land. Though the city is now only a miserable place of tents and sand hills, one day how great it will be, and we shall live to see it. The fair Golden City."

On the rude wharf stood the expectant crowd. To them the ship was the beautiful carrier-dove, with its white wings spread to bring them news of home.

"Perhaps there will be some one from the old home," said a young man, with his brown eyes filled with eager longing. "The dark old Atlantic! how its breakers used to dash upon the rocks in sight of home. It was glorious. To-morrow will be Christmas! I wonder, will they remember all, as I do!"

By his side stood a great shaggy dog, who belonged to nobody.

He talked only in the dog language, but was very learned, and understood all the young man said. He was a wonderful dog, and had his thoughts. "I am my own master," he said, "and that is pleasant—yet one likes to be cared for, and nobody cares for me. I shall get no news from home, and to-morrow will be Christmas. This is not as it should be; I must see to it."

The great dog was getting quite out of temper, and, with a surly growl, he turned round so quickly, that he gave the young man a start.

"One would think the dog was mad,' said he, "only it is not the season." Then he looked out again hopefully to the coming ship.

The great dog ran round the corner, and through the wet streets all day.

The steamer had arrived, and there were new faces looking eagerly about for old familiar ones, and the old were looking for the new; so there was altogether a great bustle such as was never seen, only in those early days when the ships came in from home. Thus the day passed, and the evening came on, raining dismally—yet it was Christmas eve.

In a dark alley sat the great dog. His shaggy coat kept him warm, yet it was very desolate there alone.

" One should have something to live for,"

growled he, "something to take care of and protect, or there is no use in being strong and brave. One might as well be a puny poodle, and sit by the parlor fire," and he gave an ugly bark, "bow, wow, wow! one should have an object in life."

Just then he heard a low moan, and looking round, he saw a poor lame dog, very thin and sick, lying down in the mud, and ready to die of hunger.

It was really quite wretched, and all the great dog's sympathies were aroused. "There *is* an object, to be sure," he said. "It is Christmas eve, and the good Santa Claus has taken pity on me, and given me this poor fellow, who needs me as much as I do him. What a zest life has, when one has something to live for."

Without any useless ceremony, he raised the poor dog, and tenderly as the mother dog carries her little ones, he bore him to a warm, dry place, and made him a nice bed of clean straw.

"This is better, my friend," said the noble creature, quite flushed and happy with the pleasure of doing a kind act. "What more can I do for you?"

"I am famishing with hunger," replied the lame dog, with a feeble groan, and off went his great shaggy protector, through rain and mud, to a restaurant, and there the cook gave him a bone, saying, " take it, you Bummer."

He caught the bone, and running off as fast as possible, in a few moments laid it before the lame dog.

It was a rich bone, and had a delicious smell that was quite reviving to the sick one.

It was so pleasant to see the poor hungry fellow eat, that Bummer could not leave him until he had finished. "I never enjoyed

a bone so much in my life," said Bummer,
as he tucked the warm straw around his
new friend, and saw him closing his eyes
with a pleasant satisfied languor.

"This is something like living," added he,
with a lively bark, as he ran back to the
restaurant for his own dinner.

"Coming again, Bummer?" said the
jolly, red-faced cook, throwing him another
bone, which he ate with a famous relish.

In the morning he went back again to
the restaurant, serving the sick dog first,
and again at night, and day after day, till
he became the jolly cook's regular pensioner.

At the restaurant they grew quite curious to know what became of the first bone,
and sent some one to follow Bummer, who
came back telling the strange story, and saying, "it is really quite wonderful."

Then every one talked of it, and soon
the whole town came to know the two

dogs, and called them Bummer and Lazarus.

In the pleasant days they walked out
together, Bummer always watching over
Lazarus with the tenderest care. It was
really a pleasant sight to see them, they
were so happy together.

Thus time passed away, making no
change in the protecting devotion of Bummer, nor the trusting love of Lazarus.

But there must be an end of all things,
and at last Lazarus died.

This was a great sorrow to poor Bummer,
and he grew so thin and wretched that the
jolly cook was quite distressed.

"You must cheer up, my good Bummer;
really it will never do; you *must* cheer up."

"It is all over now," said the dog, "one
must have something to live for. It is no
use, one must have an object."

He was no longer the Bummer of old, and

he went away to the place where Lazarus rested.

" He forgot to eat his bone," said the jolly cook; " poor fellow, we were getting used him, to and we shall miss him. He belonged to the town—he was 'our dog.'"

This was the last time he went for his bone. It was all over, and Bummer and Lazarus became a remembrance which has passed into a tradition.

The skin of Bummer was carefully stuffed, and placed in a glass case. It may still be seen in some restaurant on Montgomery Street, where it is preserved as a precious relic of the olden time.

This is a true story, little ones, and no doubt the fathers will tell you, how, in the olden days, he has often seen Bummer and Lazarus.